Fur,
Feathers,
& Scales

Fur, Feathers, & Scales

Sweet, Funny, and Strange Animal Tales

Editors
Marianne H. Donley and Carol L. Wright

BETHLEHEM WRITERS GROUP, LLC
Bethlehem, Pennsylvania, USA

Fur, Feathers, and Scales

Published by Bethlehem Writers Group, LLC
Bethlehem, Pennsylvania, USA
https://bethlehemwritersgroup.com

Copyright © 2020 by Bethlehem Writers Group, LLC

The copyright of each individual story is held by the author.

All rights reserved. No part of this book may be used or reproduced in any form, or by any electronic or mechanical means, without written permission of the copyright holder.

The contents of this publication are works of fiction. Names, characters, places, businesses, or organizations, events, and incidents are either the product of the author's imagination or used fictitiously. Any resemblance to actual persons, living or dead, organizations, events, or locales is entirely coincidental.

Front cover design: Marianne H. Donley
Print book layout and full cover design: Carol L. Wright
e-book layout: Marianne H. Donley

ISBN: 978-0-9892650-8-9 (paperback)
ISBN: 978-0-9892650-9-6 (ebook)

Images used under license from DepositPhotos.com

Library of Congress Control Number: 2020946787

Printed in the United States of America.

*For all the animals
with whom
we have shared our lives*

Also from the
BETHLEHEM WRITERS GROUP, LLC

SWEET, FUNNY, AND STRANGE ANTHOLOGIES

A Christmas Sampler:
Sweet, Funny, and Strange Holiday Tales

Once Around the Sun:
Sweet, Funny, and Strange Tales for All Seasons

A Readable Feast:
Sweet, Funny, and Strange Tales for Every Taste

Once Upon a Time:
Sweet, Funny, and Strange Tales for All Ages

Untethered:
Sweet, Funny, and Strange Tales of the Paranormal

OTHER PUBLICATIONS

Let It Snow: The Best of Bethlehem Writers Roundtable,
Winter 2015 Collection

Off the Rails: A Collection of Weird, Wicked, and Wacky
Stories by Jerome W. McFadden

Bethlehem Writers Roundtable
https://bwgwritersroundtable.com

Table of Contents

Common Knowledge 9
    A.E. Decker

Hubbard Had a Fancy Bra 25
    Brett Wolff, Winner, 2020 Short Story Award

Shingebiss 31
    Will Wright

Jack 35
    Kidd Wadsworth

Six Feet Under 53
    Dianna Sinovic

Cast Away in Seam Water 59
    Paul Weidknecht

When I Was Your Age 71
    Marianne H. Donley

Critter 73
    Diane Sismour

Buttons 81
    Ralph Hieb

Rama and the Camel 93
    Will Wright

Recycled 101
    Jerome W. McFadden

The Dignity of Man 107
    Jeff Baird

Missing the Point 119
   Emily P. W. Murphy

Inside the Tank 123
   Jodi Bogert

Man's Best Friend 131
   DT Krippene

Oranges and Roses 147
   Angela Albertson, Winner, 2019 Short Story Award

Wolf King 151
   Ralph Hieb

Why Bats Live in Caves 163
   Peter J Barbour

Goats in the Machine 167
   Christopher D. Ochs

Bease 181
   Will Wright

Fluff vs. Scales 191
   Courtney Annicchiarico

Why Children Have Their Father's Last Name . . . 201
   Marianne H. Donley

Unnatural 203
   Carol L. Wright

Tipping Point 209
   A. E. Decker

Doeg's Story 225
   Will Wright

Acknowledgements 231

About the Authors 233

Common Knowledge

A. E. Decker

The highwayman waited in a copse near the foot of Trilby Bridge. Overhead, a half-moon rode the star-flecked darkness, glinting like a coin dropped between cobbles. Tapping a finger against his saddle, the highwayman sang a soft counterpoint to the brook's gentle ripple. He loved the velvet tranquility of these moments, the open sky and the music of the water.

Rattle, clomp, creak.

The highwayman broke off his song. The noise came again, drowning the brook's susurrus: *clop, clatter, snort.* A carriage, clanking its way toward Trilby Bridge. Sighing, the highwayman knotted a black scarf over his face then patted his steed's shoulder.

"Let's get this over with," he said. "Mother's bound to chide as is."

"Stand and deliver," cried the highwayman.

The driver halted the carriage instantly. As the highwayman rode past, he sat stock-still on the box, smiling the smug smile of one whose worldly goods are not at stake. The highwayman gave him a polite nod before tapping his pistol against the carriage door. A man's florid face, framed by a grubby peruke, peered through the curtains.

"Your money," said the highwayman, leveling his pistol.

Half a minute ticked past. "Shouldn't it be 'your money or your life'?"

The highwayman shrugged. "I usually leave out the second option, since nobody ever chooses it." He waggled the pistol. "Your money, sir."

But the man's gaze listed downward. "Damn me," he said. "You're riding a unicorn." He guffawed.

The highwayman's lips tightened. "A *black* unicorn," he qualified, as if it weren't perfectly obvious, as if any twit with half a brain would set about robbing people at night on a glowingly white steed.

"A unicorn!" The *thwap* of a meaty palm slapping a fleshy thigh echoed from inside the carriage. "Tell me, lad, are the rumors true?" He leered. "Can you only ride a unicorn if you're a—"

Sighing, the highwayman reversed his grip on his pistol, swung it in an arc. *Thunk*. The florid man's eyes rolled up in their sockets. The highwayman raided his pockets, tipped his hat to the still-smirking driver, and clucked to his steed.

"That," said the unicorn as they escaped across the heath, "was more annoying than necessary."

"Yes." The highwayman didn't enjoy robbing folk, and not only because he could swing for it. But when your mother was a witch, it was wisest to bring her what she wanted, no matter the cost.

"Oh, Shay," said his mother when he presented the sandalwood oil and thirteen grams of dried bees she'd requested earlier that morning. Reproachfully, she straightened up from the cauldron she'd been stirring. Steam-damp hair fell over her cheeks.

The bitter-sharp fragrance of rosin teased Shay's nostrils. His eyes strayed to his fiddle, waiting on the corner table. He hadn't found time to play in weeks.

Thump. Shay jumped, his gaze returning to his mother as she threw the parcel onto her workbench and knuckled her fists against her hips. "When will you bring me what I need?" she demanded.

Shay stifled a groan. Last night's earnings hadn't purchased half the items she'd requested, let alone the most expensive ones. Where on earth—or, more to the point, in the town of Galding—was he going to find a ruby the size of a ha'penny?

His mother's stare no longer fixed him. She stared out the window instead, to the empty lane, eyes fierce and wild and more than a little sad. Shay glanced at his fiddle, sighed, then took up his tricorne.

The depths some folk would plummet to protect their valuables appalled Shay. Underwear was a horrifyingly popular spot for secreting jewelry. Others stuffed their cheeks with banknotes until they resembled chipmunks. And then there was the enterprising gentleman who, with Shay's pistol pointed at his face, removed his signet ring and shoved it up his own left nostril.

The trials of the highwayman lifestyle. Shay reflected while escaping across Fafner Downs after an especially aggravating heist. His latest victim had dropped a handful of guineas down his breeches, thrust out his crotch as if daring Shay to delve for them, and exclaimed, "Crikey!"

Fur, *Feathers*, and Scales

Of all the stupid words. What did it even mean? He'd had a stupid mustache, too—if it *was* a mustache. Shay preferred to believe that a caterpillar had died on his upper lip.

"You're quiet tonight," observed the unicorn.

"Just wondering why people always snigger when they see I'm riding you," said Shay.

"Look at it from their perspective," said the unicorn. Strands of his long mane flicked Shay's wrists. "You're a highwayman. A romantic figure, flourishing a *cocked* pistol while *mounted* on a beast crowned with a *long, thrusting*—"

"All right," said Shay, cheeks hot. "Don't drive the point home."

"Actually, that's exactly—"

"Don't make the obvious joke either."

They trotted in silence for a while. "So, their sniggering isn't surprising," said the unicorn. "Knowing what everyone knows about unicorns, that is."

"I suppose not," said Shay. "Knowing what everyone knows." Digging a hand into the pocket of his long coat, he brought out the evening's takings. Enough to purchase the white raven's feather and a pinch of saffron. But that left the mandrake, the speckled snakeskin, and the—

Where on earth, or out of it, was he going to find a ruby the size of a ha'penny? Did it even matter? This morning he'd brought his mother the pint of cream from a golden cow, and she'd dropped the pestle in the mortar and brushed a hand across her eyes.

"Oh, Shay," she'd said. "Do you even know what I need?"

Well, should he ever find a ha'penny-sized ruby, he'd better have the clink to purchase it. He gauged the sky. Not quite midnight; there might yet be prey about. "Let's try the bridge," he said, patting the unicorn. Trilby Bridge was his favorite, if not most lucrative, spot, with the water rippling like a trill of music beneath its graceful arch. *Music*, he thought wistfully. His fiddle would need tuning by now.

Common Knowledge

Several yards from their usual copse, the unicorn stopped. "What is it?" asked Shay.

"Somebody's there."

Shay peered through the interlocked branches. Someone indeed stood at the foot of the bridge. A smallish someone, shrouded in a black cloak, one foot tapping in a beam of moonlight. *A trap?* Shay scanned the bushes lining the road. He wasn't too worried. For all people supposedly "knew" about unicorns, it sure surprised them when his mount left pursuers' horses gasping in the dust.

No tell-tale snorts or clinking of bridles. He focused on the tapping foot, encased in a green silk boot. An heiress waiting to elope with her beau, perhaps? No matter. Shay drew his pistol from his belt. Anyone who could afford silk boots could—

Braaattzzt!

Shay glared back just as the unicorn's tail lowered. "Sorry," said the unicorn. "Shouldn't have eaten those green apples."

"I hear you, highwayman," called a voice from the vicinity of the bridge. A young lady's voice, sweet as cream with a sprinkle of nutmeg on top. "Stand and deliver."

So much for ambushing his quarry.

"I will be most cross if you don't emerge," said the young lady. A pause. "I have a pistol."

Shay cleared his throat. "Mightn't that inspire me to flee rather than approach?" he called.

"Oh." Her foot stilled. "Well, sorry. I'm not accustomed to nefarious activities." Her hood fell back, revealing a flow of red-gold hair, bright as new copper. Shay stared, enthralled. "All right, I won't shoot. Just come out, please, damn you."

Shay guided the unicorn onto the road. Moonlight revealed her pale oval face with a spattering of freckles across her nose. *Like a spray of gold dust,* thought Shay. *I'd like to kiss—count!—each one.*

The unicorn shook its mane, and Shay's mind cleared. Somewhat. "What do you want with me?" he asked, forcing a deep, gravelly tone.

"With you?" said the young lady. Even her grimace resembled a marble angel's. "Not a thing. It's your unicorn."

That threw him. "My unicorn?" he asked, his voice reverting to its usual lilt.

"Don't parrot me." Her foot resumed tapping. "Might I borrow your unicorn for one night?"

Shay studied her. The folds of her black cloak allowed glimpses of a slim-yet-curvy figure swathed in green silk. She did carry a pistol, but apparently hadn't noticed that she'd failed to cock it.

"Why?" asked Shay.

"I needn't tell you that."

"True." Shay tipped his tricorne. "Come along, George." He clucked to the unicorn. The young lady's jaw dropped as they passed her, making for the arch of Trilby Bridge. Shay counted George's steps. Fortunately, there were only five; he didn't think he could bear many more.

"Wait!" she cried, and he reined in the unicorn instantly. "I need my father to see me ride a unicorn."

Shay turned. "Again, why?"

The words spilled out in a rush. "I am Amelia Lacewood, heiress to Swardy Manor. Last week I went riding in Lord Bertie Berkenshire's coach. It broke an axle, and we were forced to spend the night in an inn and now . . . ooh!" She stamped a foot. "Father believes I'm ruined. He insists I marry Lord Berkenshire this Friday." She scrubbed an arm over her face. "I considered throwing myself from the roof. But then I recalled stories of a highwayman who rides a unicorn and I thought—well, you know what they say about unicorns."

Common Knowledge

"That they are symbol of grace and purity, granted powers to render poisoned waters potable and heal sickness?" said Shay.

Amelia shut her mouth after a moment. "Actually, I was referring to the thing everyone knows about them. You're an odd sort of highwayman, aren't you?" Her chin lifted. "Remove your mask."

Shay debated only briefly before pulling down the scarf.

"Why, you're—" Her pale cheeks bloomed.

"What?"

"Young," she said and stared ferociously at the brook.

Shay's heart did a pirouette. "Very well," he said. "You may borrow my unicorn."

The unicorn coughed, and Shay remembered himself. "For a price," he added.

"Name it," she said, folding her arms under her bosom.

The reins slipped between Shay's suddenly sweaty fingers. "You shouldn't say that. I mean, I could ask—" He couldn't finish. His face burned.

Her cheeks reddened too, but her chin rose higher. "You won't. You couldn't ride your unicorn if you did."

It was a fair piece of logic, given the common knowledge concerning unicorns. *It wouldn't be right anyway.* Shay cast about for another prize. "I don't suppose you own a ruby the size of a ha'penny?" he jested.

"Why, yes."

He stared.

"My father does, anyway. It's part of a necklace he gave to my mother on their wedding day. But I don't think he wishes to see it again, not since she died." Amelia gazed out over the brook, rubbing her arms. "He misses her so."

"She's dead? I'm so sorry. How—"

"She was bludgeoned by a swan."

"Uh."

"She was trying to feed it a rock cake."

Fur, *Feathers*, and Scales

"Ah."

"And got too close to the nest."

"Oh."

"They're vicious creatures, apparently."

"Huh." And they seemed so serene. Now he'd never be able to look at one without picturing a snake-necked killer.

"So, the ruby's yours if you want it." Her eyes, summer blue with lashes like black feathers, met his. "Can we go show my father now?"

"Now? Oh—yes. How about it, George?"

The unicorn's flank rippled in a shrug. "Fine with me."

Amelia jumped. "It talks?"

"Of course he talks. He's a unicorn." Shay raised an eyebrow as he offered her a hand. "Surely *everyone* knows that about them."

Amelia's chin went up, but she took his hand and swung into the saddle behind him. The clout she gave him with the pistol might have been accidental.

"Ow! Careful with that!"

She sniffed. "No common thief gives me orders."

"Sorry, I'm sure, miss," he muttered, trying to tamp down his pulse when she wrapped her arms around him for balance. George didn't need directions. Everyone in Galding knew where Swardy Manor lay: the biggest pile of red bricks, ivy, and half-columns in the swanky west side of town.

Half a mile passed, silent save for the three-beat rhythm of George's hooves. Then one of Amelia's hands curled over Shay's shoulder, almost tentatively. She'd tucked the pistol away, too. "George?" she asked.

Shay decided to forgive her. "It's what I call him."

George snorted. He generally avoided speaking while cantering for fear of swallowing insects.

"What's his actual name?" asked Amelia.

Common Knowledge

"Well, you click your tongue then blow out through your nose while simultaneously making a high-pitched 'eee' and shaking your head. I don't recommend trying to pronounce it; you'll get snot everywhere."

"Goodness," she said. "And what does it mean?"

"Something like 'George,' apparently. It's a common name among unicorns."

"How did you meet him?"

"I was fiddling in the woods. I mean, playing the fiddle," he clarified quickly. "He walked out between two poplars and settled down to listen. We both love music, see. One day," he said, enjoying the taste of the words, often dreamed but never before spoken aloud, "I'll live in a city by the sea, playing my fiddle as the waves wash the sand."

George's hooves beat out a full measure against the road. Then: "Why don't you earn an honest keep instead of robbing people?" she asked.

"I can't. Not until I bring my mother that ruby."

"Pooh to your mother. Be a man."

"My mother's a witch. You don't say 'pooh' to witches, even when they're your mother."

Her gasp warmed his ear. "A witch? Do you mean the witch of Habblecott Lane?"

Oh, damn. What an idiot, to let his identity slip so easily. *Maybe she won't figure it out*, he thought, but she was already speaking again.

"Mistress Iwan, that's her name. So, you're her son, Shay?"

She could have me hanged now, if she wanted. "Yes, I'm Shay," he said, absurdly happy. "Pleased to meet you, Miss Lacewood." He bowed in the saddle.

Two measures of hoof beats. Then she mimed a curtsey. "Pleased to make your acquaintance, Mr. Iwan." Her arms clasped his waist again. "Why does your mother need a ruby?"

"It's the final component for the spell she's concocting." He hoped it was the final component, at least.

"What kind of spell?"

"I believe it's a spell for happiness." Ironic that, considering how miserable its creation was making him.

Up ahead, gray and sooty in the moonlight, the great cube of Swardy Manor loomed, surrounded by grass trimmed to a half-inch and bushes clipped into perfect spheres, like giant toffee apples stuck into the ground.

"A spell," said Amelia. She shifted against his back. "If I could do magic, I'd grow a pair of wings and fly away from Galding. Perhaps I'd find happiness in your city by the sea."

This had never occurred to Shay. "You're not happy?" he asked as they clopped up Swardy Manor's beech-lined drive.

"Happy?" Her voice hit a perfect high G of horror. "With every middle-aged rake and chinless second son from here to Hubblesworth wooing me? Why, Lord Berkenshire's the prize calf among them, and he has a horrid mustache and says 'Crikey' all the time."

George froze, one hoof poised inches from the white gravel.

"'Crikey.' What does that even—is something wrong?" She tugged at his arm. "You've gone very still. Gads, your hair's wavy. I could curl it about my finger."

Shay cleared his throat. "No," he said, carefully. "Nothing's wrong. We will continue up the drive, your father will watch you ride George, and you will absolutely never marry that bast—Lord Berkenshire on Friday. Right, George?"

George licked his lips. "Right." He set the hoof down.

They continued up the drive. A coach was drawn up in front of the wide expanse of marble steps; a hideous contraption, black-and-gold, like a melodramatic bumblebee. Amelia's arms stiffened around him. Shay stiffened, too.

Common Knowledge

"That's Lord Berkenshire's coach," they said simultaneously.

"You know Lord Berkenshire?" said Amelia.

"I robbed him an hour before I met you," he whispered, guiding George to the shelter of a spiral-cut shrubbery.

"Good."

"No, it isn't." Shay rubbed his temples. "We must alter our plans."

"Why?"

"Because if you call to your father to watch you ride a unicorn, Lord Berkenshire will come too, and he might recognize me."

"Yes, I was going to mention that tying a hanky over the lower half of your face isn't exactly an impenetrable disguise. Especially when one's eyes are so pretty a violet as yours."

His heart fluttered. "Do you really think—"

George coughed. Shay hastily steered his thoughts back on course. "Maybe you could slip inside and get the ruby," he said. "Then you can slip back out and give it to me. I'll cut home across Fafner Downs. Give me ten minutes' start before you call your father out."

He twisted in the saddle to look at her. She was nodding and biting her lip. "All right?" he asked.

"What about George?"

"Don't worry about me." George nibbled the shrubbery. "I can find my own way home after you ride me."

"Is it all right?" Shay asked again when she remained silent a long minute. "Are you worried about slipping into the house?"

"No, I can do that. I just realized." Her teeth dug into her lip again. "Everything will return to the way it was before the axle broke."

"Isn't that what you want?"

"Oh, it's all very well for you," she said in an angry whisper. A tear rolled off her chin and splashed onto his collar. "You have your city by the sea." She slid off George's back, lips tight as a knotted ribbon. "I'll return with the ruby in three minutes."

What was that about? Shay watched, frowning, as she tiptoed to a side door and vanished inside. Habit then drew his gaze toward Lord Berkenshire's coach. Lord Berkenshire's *gilded* coach. Shay smarted at the memory of the fat handful of guineas he'd dropped down his crotch. "Bet there's a chest hidden under the cushions," he said.

"Don't think about it," said George through a mouthful of leaves.

"I'm not." He was. No coachman in sight. Shay's fingers itched. It would be so *easy*. And Lord Berkenshire deserved a good robbing.

Shay's legs ached from riding, so he dismounted to stretch them. Perfectly sensible. Walking stretched them even better. Idly, he closed the distance to the coach by ten feet.

Voices inside the house. Shay strained his ears, trying to make out words while his feet sidled him closer to the coach. His fingertips brushed the latch.

A door creaked. The rapid patter of footsteps followed. Startled, Shay threw himself into the nearest hiding spot: beneath the coach. His belly scraped the raked gravel as footsteps scrunched closer.

"Shay," hissed a voice, a cream-with-nutmeg voice.

Amelia. Shay sat up and banged his head on the axle. "Ow."

"Shay?" Amelia's face appeared in the gap between gravel and coach bottom. "What are you doing down there?"

The axle. Frowning, Shay squinted at it, rubbing his head. "Hey." He crawled out.

Common Knowledge

Amelia clutched a gem red as all the wine in the world. Grass, carriage, and drive all took on a rosy hue after looking at it. "Your payment," she said, offering it.

"Thank you." Shay held the jewel a while longer than necessary, admiring its cold fire and trying not to calculate how many days' board it might purchase in a city by the sea. Becoming aware of Amelia's stare, he hastily stowed it in a pocket. "Were you inside the coach when the axle broke?" he asked.

"No, we were dining at the inn," said Amelia. "The coachman informed Lord Berkenshire it was broken. Why?"

"Because I know about coaches—part of my job—and neither of those axles has been replaced recently."

Amelia stared. Every drop of color leeched from her face. "He smiled when the coachman told him about the axle," she whispered.

Shay wrapped an arm around her shoulders. "Go to your father," he said. "Tell him—"

Bang. Swardy Manor's front door slammed open, throwing a rectangle of yellow light over them. "Lord Lacewood," called a man at the top of the marble steps, "the highwayman's here now, abducting your daughter."

"George," cried Shay, darting toward his steed. But the man lunged down the steps and blocked his way. Two feet of polished steel pressed against Shay's windpipe. Shay's gaze travelled the blade's length to settle on a dead-caterpillar mustache. He tried not to swallow.

George whinnied, pawing the ground. "Stay back, unicorn," said Lord Berkenshire. The sword bit deeper. "Your rider will live longer." He laughed. "Long enough to hang, anyway. How pitiful, dying a vir—"

Amelia's foot came up between Lord Berkenshire's legs. Something in his groin clanked; he must've forgotten a few guineas. His eyes crossed. The sword dropped from his hand.

"You planned it all," she raged. "You beast!"

A "crikey" might have been blooming on Lord Berkenshire's lips, but she hit him over the head with the butt of her pistol before it emerged. He crumpled to the ground, emitting small whining noises. Shay grabbed Amelia before she kicked him again.

"You can prove him a liar," he said. "Ride George."

"No, you ride him."

"What? Why?" asked Shay as Amelia woman-handled him onto George's back.

"Weren't you listening? My father believes you're abducting me, so—" She looked up. Shay followed her gaze. High on the roof, a tall man leapt onto the back of some large creature. Its spread wings blotted out the moon.

"That's a griffin," said Shay. Surprisingly, his voice didn't shake.

"Yes, Gina." Amelia scrambled up behind him. "And that's Father on her back."

"You didn't tell me he has a griffin," said Shay as the conjoined figures leapt off the roof, descending toward them at an alarming rate.

"I didn't see a need." The shadow of the griffin fell across them. Curved beak and wicked claws. "Go, George," she cried. George leapt forward.

"Head for Mother's," added Shay as the griffin swooped. The gust of its passage raised hairs on his head. "This is hardly the way to convince him I'm not abducting you," he called to Amelia over the rush of wind.

"He must see me riding a unicorn."

"He's seen you! Now you can—"

A second swoop tore Shay's tricorne off his head. He gave up the argument. Ducking low over George's neck, he urged him to a faster pace. The unicorn's hooves scraped sparks off the cobbles.

The weight of the ruby burned in Shay's pocket. At least he could bring his mother what she needed before he fled Galding.

They turned down Habblecott Lane. Lamps glowed in the windows of his mother's house, waiting at the end. The griffin swooped again, and Lord Lacewood jumped off its back, landing neatly on his feet, a drawn sword in one hand.

"Hurry," Shay told George.

"I am hurryi—*phagh!* Gah, you made me swallow a fly."

The house at the end of the lane grew in perspective from a dollhouse to a real, two-storied building, its snowy façade laced with climbing roses. George pulled up, panting, and Shay dragged Amelia off his back and bundled her into the house, Lord Lacewood ten steps behind.

Shay slammed the door. "Mother," he said, expecting to discover her at the counter, ladle or pestle in hand. Instead, she sat at the table, which was spread with a fine linen cloth and laden with silver dishes. Beeswax candles flickered. A heavenly fragrance of saffron, wine, and roast pheasant ennobled the air.

"Mother?" Shay gaped.

The door behind him burst open. Lord Lacewood strode inside, his strong face lined, but handsome. "Unhand my daughter," he commanded, lifting his sword.

Shay's mother rose, smiling. She wore her finest dress, the garnet red one. Her glossy black hair showed only the slightest traces of gray as it cascaded over her shoulders. "Finally, Shay," she said, extending her hand to Lord Lacewood. "You brought me what I need."

Lord Lacewood met her eyes. His sword's tip dropped, brushing the braided rug. When he reached out, the air between their fingertips crackled with electricity.

They clasped.

Fur, *Feathers,* and Scales

Neither noticed when Shay retrieved his fiddle from the corner table. Amelia waited outside, tears soaking her smile. "I don't think he'll be lonely anymore," she said.

Shay closed the door on the tableau. "I thought she needed this," he said, taking the ruby from his pocket. Amelia plucked it from his grasp. Before he could protest, she slipped back inside, placed the gem in her father's hand, and folded his fingers around it.

"It was the final ingredient for your mother's spell, wasn't it?" she asked, shutting the door behind her.

Yes, and it would set off her gown perfectly, gleaming in the hollow of her throat. But—

"I could've lived off that gem for years," he said.

She swatted his shoulder. "You must become an honest man if you wish me to stay." Hoisting herself onto George's back, she sat demurely sidesaddle, her hands folded in her lap.

Shay collected his jaw. "You're coming with me?"

"It may not be a pair of wings, but riding a black unicorn possesses a certain panache."

"I've always thought so," said George.

Amelia patted George's rump in invitation. Shay leapt up behind her and wrapped his arms around her waist. She readjusted his grip.

"Don't be naughty," she said, softening the reproof with a peck on his cheek. "You wouldn't be able to ride George anymore."

Shay smiled into her hair. No hurry. They'd have time together in the city by the sea. Time, and the happiness promised by his mother's spell.

Soon enough, he suspected, she'd be delighted to learn—as a few lasses in Galding had—why one should not always trust the common knowledge when it came to unicorns.

Hubbard Had a Fancy Bra

Brett Wolff
Winner, 2020 Short Story Award

Hubbard had a fancy bra, which was odd. Hubbard didn't need a fancy bra. There was nothing about Hubbard for which a bra, of any sort, made sense. Hubbard was a raccoon and rarely needed lingerie.

On this particular evening, however, Hubbard discovered the delicate lace object waving frantically in the wind, hooked on a rotting set of stairs in back of the old Henson farm. No other clothing was present as far as Hubbard could see, and he had excellent night vision. He was a raccoon, after all.

Normally, Hubbard would have left the dangling unmentionable where it had been dangling and not thought twice about it. But this particular item had an unusually pleasant aroma. It was, without overstating it, hypnotic in its allure. It didn't smell at all of Hubbard's standard fare—garbage. Instead, it smelled sweet, crisp, and downright floral.

Hubbard grabbed one of the dome-shaped cups in his tiny little hands and licked the pale fabric. It did not taste like flowers. It was clearly not food, but it inspired a sense of something he didn't quite understand.

Hubbard was quite deep, as raccoons go, and prone to extended fits of contemplation, which often left him the last in line for food among his ravenous peers. Hubbard was a picky eater. Garbage as food always felt wrong, like somehow raccoons were lesser animals. Hubbard didn't feel lesser at all.

And this was something else, entirely. The light blue bra fluttered enticingly in the wind. Hubbard watched.

What really is the point here? he thought.

He was unable to simply tread away. Hubbard grabbed a flapping strap with one paw and pulled the bra fully free of the snag upon which it was hooked.

As the bra flopped ingloriously to the ground, he heard a voice yelling. It was human. Definitely a human female, no doubt. Humans were the loud ones. They were essentially harmless, given a wide enough berth, but very large and annoyingly obstreperous.

This voice came closer and closer. This particular human seemed capable of light, and Hubbard watched as a fan of light danced across the field just the other side of the Henson's collapsed post-hole fence.

"Johnny!" the human female shouted. "I am going to kill you. What the hell did you do with it?"

"Leave it be, Cinny! You'll never find it. It's gooonnnee with the wiiinnnnd!" a human male's voice bellowed, then laughed menacingly.

Such loud creatures. It's the middle of the night. This is raccoon time, not human time, Hubbard pondered.

Hubbard moved cautiously out of the way of the serpentine spotlight and under a nearby short set of stairs. He moved the bra strap to his mouth to allow him to move more quickly, having not yet committed to his plan for it.

With humans, it was generally best to give them their space. They were unpredictable. He backed up into the crawlspace under the derelict farmhouse and settled in to watch.

Hubbard Had a Fancy Bra

"Hubbard?" a voice behind him asked. "What are you doing?"

Startled, Hubbard turned to see the soft furry face of Margery, and his heart thumped a bit. Unfortunately, the dark, wide eyes of Margery's ever-present friend and unrepentant omnivore, Tina, were also staring back from behind a flank of cobwebs.

Tina was standing mostly in front of Margery, with a disapproving look on her face, one that seemed painted into her furry coloring.

"Hi, Tina," Hubbard responded unenthusiastically with a touch of a lisp, as the bra strap dangled in his mouth. Hubbard smiled shyly toward Margery. The bra hid his intended smile—but then, so did his fur.

"What's that you are dragging around?" Tina asked.

"Um. I found it. It's mine," he said not sure why he felt embarrassed—or possessive. It was just a bra. But it was a fancy bra.

"What's that smell?" Tina asked.

"Nothing."

The human's light hit the stairs, and all three raccoons turned and froze, staring directly into the light. The female called Cinny wandered by, half-dressed—the bottom half.

Just then the storm fully broke loose all over again.

The fuzzy threesome watched the human carefully, as she sought cover under the burned-out awning just few steps away. Cinny wrapped her arms around her shoulders against the warm, wet wind.

"Johnny! I'm going to kill you!" she shouted, seemingly at no one.

Margery turned toward Hubbard and smiled. "That smells really good," she said softly, nodding supportively. Hubbard melted into the soft dirt.

But his smile was—again—thwarted, as Tina caught the moment out of the corner of her ever-vigilant eyes and sighed. "I'm sure it belongs to that human out there. Now that you've brought it in here with us, I'm sure it's going to come in looking for it. I'd drop it and get out of here if I were you. Come along, Margery. I'm going to dig over in the pile of leaves the wind is blowing against the house." Tina turned and glared at Margery, imploringly.

"I'll be over in a bit," Margery responded. "Save me a spot out of the rain."

"Your loss when I find something good," Tina grumbled and ambled out from under the house, her fur rocking across her haunches in two directions at once.

Tina's movement caught the edge of Cinny's light, and she bent down and saw Hubbard and Margery, their eyes reflecting back. "Johnny, bring me a stick or something. I think a couple of raccoons took off with my bra."

"I have the shotgun in the truck," Johnny yelled. "I'm hunting wabbits..."

"Maybe just to scare them off," Cinny shouted back. She bent down and panned the light back and forth. "You little rascals. Gimme that back." She laughed. "What the hell do you want with my bra?"

Hubbard moved forward a bit, blocking the light from Margery. Any escape was now cut off.

Cinny walked around looking for a stick or some means of poking under the house. She discovered that she had a few wrapped-up mints in her pocket. She bent down and unwrapped two and held them on her flat hand in front of the light. "Here, guys. Sweet treats. Yum, yum. I'll trade ya." She laughed again and threw the candies a few feet away.

Hubbard and Margery watched the mints land and bounce, but neither flinched.

Johnny rounded the corner of the farmhouse with his shotgun and a huge smile. A flash of lighting was followed almost immediately by a bang of thunder, causing Johnny to drop his gun into a big mud puddle. "Jesus. That was close," he shouted as he tried to fish his gun from the murky water without stepping fully into it.

Cinny abandoned the pretense of covering up and went back to wandering the yard, accepting the dampness was a fait accompli. "That was my best bra, you dumbass. It's now under the house."

Johnny laughed as he was shaking the water out of his gun. "Dang it, I'm going have to spend hours cleaning this thing. Cinny, it's coming down cats and dogs out here. Forget about the damn bra. Let's go back to the truck, girl!"

Johnny tried to climb over the fence with one hand holding his gun, just as a huge gust of wind kicked up. The force pushed him into a snappy little juniper bush, which collapsed as he fell into it. "Crap!"

Cinny turned the light in his direction, shining it in his eyes. "Yes! You deserved that!" she shouted.

"Damn it," he said, laughing and holding his hands up, attempting to block the light from his eyes.

"You're beaming me, girl," he said, struggling to extricate himself from the vituperative foliage. Cinny mocked him by shining the light constantly in his eyes, laughing herself.

"What? What? You mean like this?" She waved the light at his face.

"Stop that. I can't see."

Cinny came just within reach, and Johnny reached forward and grabbed the flashlight. Cinny playfully struggled briefly before giving up the light and running away. A few steps off, she turned back and stood with her hands on her hips, tauntingly.

Johnny got to his feet and shone the light on her half-naked, soaking wet body.

"Oh, my god, girl. Look at you. You look amazing," he said softly.

Fur, *Feathers*, and Scales

The words washed over Cinny with more impact than the howling wind.

"Johnny. Stop," she whispered, her eyes twinkling in reflection.

Johnny strode forward, dropped his light into a nearby puddle and grabbed her forcefully. She reached up and threw her arm around his neck. Their kiss was deep and desperate. Their arms and legs fought each other for a good grip on damp skin.

After a few intense moments, they flopped onto the soft ground, splashing into muddy water. Grunts and groans quickly overcame splashing and flopping, unconcerned as to the sullied waves lapping around them.

From under the old house, Hubbard made his way over to the mints lying in the dirt and picked one up in his paws. He made his way back to Margery and set the mint in front of her. Hubbard and Margery watched the two rowdy animals rutting in the mud nearby with rapt attention, taking turns licking the mint.

The saturated floorboard above them began dripping water onto their heads, but neither flinched and neither wanted to move away. Hubbard felt Margery nestle closer to him. He realized he still had the bra strap in his mouth and flipped his head a bit to upend the lacy cups onto the ground in front of them. The two pre-formed domes presented a lovely little shelter for two, and Margery moved forward, sliding her head under one side. Hubbard rustled forward into the other side right next to her, allowing the fancy bra to form a beautiful double umbrella and barrier from the dribbling rivulets from above.

The two raccoons settled into the soft dirt, side by side, watching Johnny and Cinny roll and grind back and forth in the mud.

Hubbard and Margery shared a fancy bra, and it wasn't odd at all.

Shingebiss

Will Wright
(Adapted from the Ojibwa tale)

Short winter days on Great Lake Huron
The North Wind reigns as chief of all
Forcing Man and wolf and hare and deer on
To places sheltered from icy squall
To den and cave and warming hall

In his tent by the lakeside cozy
Lived the brown duck, Shingebiss
When feathers ruffled or cheeks were rosy
He laid four logs on the fire to hiss
Four large logs for winter's bliss

At dawn the duck would do his fishing
Braving cold and frost of hoar
And if for warmth his heart was wishing
He'd go home and set on floor
A merry fire with his large logs, four

The Wind Chief saw the one tent standing
Near where lakeside rushes grow
In appearance like a summer landing
With holes for fishing in a row
"This duck, this Shingebiss must go!

Fur, *Feathers,* and Scales

"He doesn't shudder, he's never wheezing
He refuses to the southlands fly
His fishing holes then, I'll be freezing
So he'll have no food nearby
Without fish, Shingebiss will die."

Shingebiss told the North Wind Chief
"You're just a creature, much like me
Though you may cause much toil and grief
I will not fear you, so I'm free."
Shingebiss cut new fishing holes, three

Each day the duck cut holes to fish
And dared the North Wind's mighty howling
And caught as much as he might wish
To sustain and keep the bold young fowl
Lingering through the winter's growling

"This little duck, he does not fear me
I am the Chief," the North Wind cried
"Yet he would fear if he were near me."
So lifting flap, he came inside
To blow on Shingebiss till he died

The Wind Chief loosed an icy chill
That whispered thoughts both dire and dread
With malice cold enough to kill
But Shingebiss calmly turned his head
Though he could not see the wind, he said

"I know who sets my tent a-blowing
You're still a creature, much like me
With all your ice and wind and snowing
I will not fear you, so I'm free."
He stirred the fire and let things be

Shingebiss

The Chief blew harder, though not colder
Blowing feathers, fur, and hair
It raised the fire from its smolder
The four logs burned with flame and flair
The duck smelled changes in the air

The Wind felt drops of water dripping
From his newly fevered brow
Silent tears from cold eyes tipping
That never felt a tear till now
"How can I cry? I don't know how."

"Don't you see, you've stayed too long
Winter's passing as you sit.
Butterflies and birds of song
From budding branches fly and flit."
With a feeble breeze, the North Wind quit

In dark December and months beyond
On Huron's shores, brave ducks you see
With fishing holes in lakes and pond
Like their father Shingebiss they be
Never fearing, always free.

Jack

Kidd Wadsworth

"Mom, I don't want a dog."

She points to the long row of cages. "What's the harm in looking? We're already here."

"Would you like to see the dogs in the next building?" our guide asks. She seems to bounce from place to place. Maybe she's wearing those shoes, the kind with springs in the heel. Yeah, right. Maybe she's sixteen, and no one's beaten her yet.

I've divided my life into two parts: the before part—before my husband beat me and left me to die, and the after part—which includes panic attacks, flashbacks, nightmares, and, of course, the ever-wonderful walking. My feet don't exactly do as they're told. As Mom and the beautiful, naïve fool walk out the back door, my right foot makes one of its more unique decisions.

"Shit!"

I grab at a cage on my way down, landing hard on my hip. At least, no one sees me fall—no one, meaning Mom. Of course, there isn't really anyone else. Hey, want to find out who your friends are? Go through eighteen months of intensive physical therapy and see who still phones.

I suppose I should be angry at my husband. After all, he beat me. But I'm not. I'm mad at God. I'd prayed before

Fur, *Feathers*, and Scales

I'd decided to marry Mark. I'd even followed the no-sex-before-the-wedding rule.

So, I figure it wasn't really Mark who betrayed me, it was God. He hadn't warned me. No, it was much worse than that. God set a trap for me. Mark: handsome, great job, I'd even met him at church. And now that I'm hurt? Where is God? Guess He's on vacation: Venus, Jupiter, Messier 82?

Hey, I'm still here. Remember, me? I'm the one lying on the floor of the Tri-City Animal Shelter.

At first, when I woke up in the hospital, I prayed that God would send me an angel, someone to heal me, to help me. Now, I pray to die. I want to confront God. I imagine myself shoving St. Peter aside, marching through the pearly gates, past the angelic choirs and into the smoke-filled throne room. I'd scream at him, "*Why!*"

I lie on the floor, my cheek pressed against the cold linoleum, waiting to die.

I open my eyes. Nope, not dead.

Instead, I'm eye level with a beagle, cowering in the back of his cage. He's painfully small, with a mangled, half-torn-off ear; his coat lacks any sort of shine. Crisscrossing his right forepaw, a long cut glares, covered with a fresh, juicy scab. Other scars, some old, some new, have me hating God all over again.

A dog? You let this happen to an innocent animal? You're not a God of love. You're a God of cruelty.

The beagle's eyes find mine. Head down in subservience, the pup crawls toward me, whimpering. My right hand is pressed up and twisted against the cage. Twice he reaches out a paw but draws back.

I whisper, "I'll never hurt you."

Again, he reaches out. The sandpaper bottom of his paw touches my hand . . .

. . . and the world changes.

Jack

I peer out from under a chair at a room slightly out of focus. I blink, trying to see: beige carpet, ugly yellow Formica in the kitchen.

What?

Scents flood my nose: cigarette smoke, reeking, like I have my nose pressed up against an ashtray. Body odor—the stench of his sweat could only be worse if I had my nose crammed into his armpit. Carpet smells of tracked-in car exhaust and dust explode into the air as he walks; dryer sheet smells burst from his jeans. I swear I could close my eyes and follow his movements with my nose.

Blissful scents rise from the trash can: Micky D's scrambled eggs, hot cakes, sausage, maple syrup, and, not so blissful, oily margarine. I'm hungry, so hungry.

Sounds are different, too. The refrigerator emits a constant squeal. Outside, the low rumble of a car interspersed with a rattle tells me the neighbor's door will open soon. The jingle of keys. I cringe waiting for it—the jarring creak of the hinges. Bang, the door shuts.

Think.

I was in the animal shelter. I fell; saw the dog; it touched me.

Is this death? Is this what I asked for? Is God granting my wish in a way I never imagined?

Take a deep breath. . . .

My ribs hurt. My ear stings. I stretch out my hand—it's a paw.

Is this some cruel joke, some Twilight Zone episode? Am I the dog?

Blood pounds in my ears.

Stop. Stop panicking. Nothing could be as bad as Mark.

Snap! The sour tang of Coors Light overwhelms my nose.

It's more than seeing through the beagle's eyes. I know what he knows. It's knowledge without words. Or maybe, knowledge that I must give words to. I grapple with an emotion, trying to name it . . . dread.

More words come—

I've got to get out of here.

More knowledge—more words.

Oh, God. He's a "Mark." Cruel, like my husband.

I know what he's going to do. My aching body tells me. I pull in my legs, making myself as small as possible.

It won't work. It never works.

The door . . . maybe it's open.

I turn . . . it's shut.

It's always shut.

With a lazy stride, boot heels scuffing the carpet, he ambles closer.

The scent of dog sweat, my sweat, fills my nose. Panic rips through me. Hoping for pity, I whimper.

Is this how animals feel? Oh, God. The beagle went through this powerless, without even words to rage at you.

The man kicks over the chair. Beer sloshes from the can onto me, burning as it hits my slashed ear. The pointed toe of a cowboy boot swings rapidly toward me. I jump, but my leg doesn't work well. Of course, it doesn't. I'm injured. The man has kicked him—kicked me—so many times before.

"Stupid mutt!"

The boot hits me. Pain sears through my left side. My shoulder collides with a stereo speaker.

I return to reality—to the shelter, to a world in focus, to only one scent: disinfectant. I jerk backward, sliding across the room until my back finds the wall. Gulping in air, I touch my body, raise my hands—my wonderful, human hands—in front of my face.

Jack

I look into his soft, brown eyes. "You . . . you showed me."

He whimpers.

"You're trying to tell me what happened to you. I understand." Sliding back across the floor I try to make my voice as small and gentle as I can. "I understand; I really do." But as I push my index finger into the cage, he scurries back against the wall.

"No, don't be afraid. I heard you. I heard your pain."

Slowly, he inches forward, stretching out a paw. We touch, this time without the Twilight Zone effects. A shiver runs through me, raising chill bumps on my arm. I lie full on the floor, stretching out. He stretches out, too. I can only get one finger through the cage. I rub it along the top of his head and partway down his back.

Behind me, the outside door opens. Mom runs to me.

"I'm okay. Really." I smile up at her. "Mom, I'd like to adopt this dog."

"Oh, he's a rescue," the teen says. "I'm not sure he's well enough to be adopted."

"Please, let's find out. And if he's not, I'll wait for him."

The vet's reservations are not about his physical condition. "His wounds are healing well. But emotionally . . ."

"Trust me. I've got this."

Mom takes care of the necessities: a leash, a doggy car-carrier, a red doggy bowl covered with white paw prints, a white water bowl covered with red doggy prints, a flannel-lined doggy bed, dog food.

On the way home—she's driving, I'm not approved to drive—she asks, "What's his name, sweetie?"

"He doesn't have a name, Mom. Because he doesn't have any words." Tears stream down my face. "He didn't have words to cry out. Oh, God, Mom, he went through it alone. He was all alone."

Fur, *Feathers,* and Scales

At a stoplight, she reaches in her purse and pulls out a packet of tissues. "How about Jack?"

When I get home, I gently set Jack's doggy carrier on the floor and open the door. Mom politely excuses herself to visit my bathroom. When she emerges, she has in her hand the pad of paper I keep in my medicine cabinet listing the times I've taken each of my five medications. Obviously, there is an entry missing.

"Chrissy, did you take your medicine this morning?"

Why did I let her inside my apartment?

"Sweetie, you can't keep forgetting."

I try not to shout. "Mom, I know."

"Why don't I set an alarm on your phone."

"I'll set it."

She picks up my purse and takes out my phone. "What's your password, sweetie?"

I stumble across the room and grab my phone out of her hand. "I can do it."

"I'm just trying to help."

"Leave."

When the door shuts behind her, I collapse onto the carpet, not even making it to a chair. Yup, forgot the medicine. Five, or is it fifteen minutes later, I crawl to the bathroom and gulp it down.

It takes hours for me to recover. Finally, back in the living room, I reach for my phone to set a take-your-medicine alarm.

Where is he?

"Jack? Jack?"

Jack

With a wildly beating heart, I search the room. Then bending down look under the furniture, relief floods through me: He's under the couch.

"Of course, you're hiding. Got it."

I cross the room and lie down on the carpet, trying to touch him. My arm isn't quite long enough, because he's wedged himself into the corner.

"I saw what you showed me. I understand. It happened to me, too."

He makes up the distance between us, reaching out a paw . . .

. . . and the world changes. Only this time, I see my own past. I see Mark.

So different from the last vision, this one is in focus. I always loved the way Mark's dark hair fell into his eyes. He's wearing a bright blue polo shirt, Dockers pants, and the leather boat shoes I bought him for Christmas. I know what's coming, but I'm strangely calm. Maybe because I've seen this movie before. I've got the ending memorized. The smells are muted, but I notice them more now, especially the smell of his sweat. Beads of it dot his forehead.

Why is he sweating? The air conditioning is on. Oh, he's high.

I scream, "I want a divorce."

He's shaking, his hands clenched into fists. "You want! I don't give a damn what you want!"

He's between me and the bedroom door. My eyes dart to the window.

"Thinking of jumping? Two floors? Onto the concrete patio?"

Maybe I should have. Maybe breaking my pelvis would have been better than the head injury he gave me. At least, I would have gotten medical attention immediately. I wouldn't have lain on the carpet for five hours until Mom grew so worried, she'd used her key.

He grabs my hair.

I scream as he jerks me backward, then forward, ramming my face into his knee. Pain shoots through my nose.

Why didn't my neighbor call the police? She was home. Not ten minutes before, I'd waved to her as she'd watered her plants on her balcony. She hadn't even bothered to knock on the door after Mark left. Months later I saw her again, when I moved out. She hadn't said a word. She must have heard me scream, and she'd done nothing.

Again, I scream. He throws me; my head hits the corner of the nightstand.

The door opens and slams shut, the sound echoing in my head like a thousand doors slamming closed on a thousand things I'll never do again. Slam: You'll never walk without a limp. Slam: You'll never hear a high-pitched sound in your right ear. Slam: You'll never be able to control your right foot.

Relief melts through me. *He's gone.*

I'll call Mom; she'll help me.

The carpet under my face grows warm and wet. I can't see.

Why can't I see? Where did I leave my phone?

"Chrissie, can you hear me? Chrissie, Chrissie, please, Chrissie, please wake up. . . ." Mom fumbles for her phone. "I need an ambulance. It's my daughter. I think her husband has killed her. He's murdered my baby." She weeps. She kisses me. "Please don't be dead. Please. I love you."

I snap back into reality, staring into Jack's beautiful eyes. "Did that really happen? Did she say that?"

Jack

Jack crawls out from under the couch and Eskimo kisses me.

"Not the answer I was looking for, but I'll take it."

We decide to spend some time out on my back patio. Okay, I decide to sit on my back patio. I force myself to work on my lesson plans. The tears come. My mom is the only one who thinks I'll ever be able to teach second grade again.

Doesn't she get it, that I'm broken? That I'm afraid to sit on my patio? What happens if I get a panic attack in the classroom?

I'd left the sliding glass door open. About an hour into my pathetic attempt to edit my lesson plans, a small noise tells me that Jack has decided to venture out, probably for a bathroom break. I don't turn. He sure doesn't need me watching his every move. I'm not my mother. Two hours later, I've completed one and only one lesson plan. *Wow.*

"Jack, time for dinner."

The sound of paws trotting across the carpet surprises me.

"You came." I almost pick him up, but with his injuries, I curb my need. Instead, I pat his head.

"How about some food, boy?" I pour some dog food into his brand-new doggy bowl. He backs away, lies down on the floor, and stares at it.

"What's wrong, boy? Wrong kind of food?"

I sit beside him and wait.

"Show me," I whisper.

He touches me with his paw . . .

 . . . and my kitchen disappears.

Perhaps the previous vision should have prepared me, but seeing through Jack's eyes is so different. A blurry stove and refrigerator, and the scents, the wonderful scents are everywhere. I'm in scent heaven. I lie on my belly on the cold floor staring at a light blue doggy bowl, filled to the brim. Spit drips out of my eager mouth. I sniff in beef tongue, fat and blood, chicken gizzards, and turkey. My empty belly aches. The man moves, bringing to my nose his scents of leather and sticky hair gel.

I freeze. I know he's right behind me.

The wound on my paw itches. Trembling, I dare to lick it.

Reaching over me, he stirs the food with his finger, intensifying the heady fragrance of meat, luscious meat.

"Oh, sorry mutt. I forgot."

He moves to the sink, pours water on the food, and again stirs it.

The magnificent scents are so heavy in the air, I can taste the food. I whimper and move toward the bowl.

Stepping over me, he scoots it away with toe of his boot.

"You want this? Yeah, I bet you do."

Shaking with need, I wait.

He opens the refrigerator. Its annoying squeal becomes deafening. More wonderful scents: pizza, tacos, cheese, bacon beginning to rot. He reaches inside, his back to me and the bowl.

Totally silent, I inch forward.

He turns, picks up the bowl and puts it on top of the refrigerator.

"Aw . . . too bad."

Bending down, the man waves a slice of pizza in front of my face—sausage, spicy pepperoni, cheese. Better still, his hand: warm flesh, pulsing with blood. . . .

"You want this, mutt?"

Jack

. . . and the kitchen reappears.

"I hope you bit his hand off."

Jack looks up at me with totally innocent eyes.

"Yeah, don't give me that look. I know. I used to dream of hiring some dude in prison to beat up Mark. I'd tell him to make sure he rammed Mark's head into a pointed object and left him to bleed out."

Mom had restocked the fridge this morning, before she'd insisted that I get out of the apartment, before she'd arrogantly decided I needed a dog. As I open the refrigerator, I find myself wondering if it, too, has an annoying high-pitched squeal I can't hear.

I find freshly sliced, oven-gold turkey from the deli counter. That will do. Calling to Jack, we go into the living room. I sit on the couch. Gently, I lean forward and pick him up, settling him beside me. Carefully, I put the turkey in my open palm. Keeping my fingers back, well out of the way, I watch as he gobbles it down. Later, when I pour water in his bowl, he doesn't hesitate to lap it up.

The days fly by. Jack likes detective shows, especially snarling at villains. He always knows who did it.

Mom visits daily, checking up on me. "Did you take your medicine?"

"Yes, Mom."

"Maybe you should go out for lunch."

"It's more nutritious to eat at home."

Jack now greets my mother with yelps of joy, no doubt because she brings him gourmet dog food and today, sliced London broil.

"Maybe you and Jack should go to the dog park. Jack needs exercise, sweetie. It will help his wounds heal."

I look down into his wonderfully kind eyes.

There will be other people at the dog park. "I don't know . . ."

"I'll come with you."

Fur, *Feathers*, and Scales

We couldn't have dreamed up a more wonderful day. Jack is a natural at frisbee. He chases butterflies, rolls in the grass, eats a cricket.

That evening, Jack pushes open the bathroom door while I'm in the shower. He puts his paws on the side of the tub.

I peek around the shower curtain. "What's up, boy?"

He reaches out a paw to touch my wet leg. I wait, but the world doesn't change. On a whim, I turn the shower to barely warm, and bring him in with me. He yelps and squirms, trying to lick the water. I put him down in the tub. I've got a slow drain, but I don't relish letting the apartment's handyman in. My abode is strictly a man-free zone. I've tried drain cleaner and all sorts of little, plastic, drain-cleaning wands Mom brings me, but I still spend the latter half of every shower in ankle-deep water. Now, as the tub slowly fills, Jack whacks the water with his tail. He licks it. He jumps against the side of the tub, slides down, and belly flops. I decide against lathering up. Don't want to get soap in his puppy eyes. I'll do a little spot-cleaning later in the sink. Probably best to shampoo my hair there, too.

Ruff. Ruff.

"Do you know that you have a happy bark?"

Ruff. Ruff.

I lift him up into the stream. He licks my face, and for the first time in eighteen months, I laugh.

Two days later, Mom shows up at my apartment with clothes. Yes, she's decided to tell me how to dress. I rip into her. "Really? You don't think I can dress myself anymore?"

"Well, you have a tendency to look a little frumpy."

"Frumpy?"

Jack

She gives my two-sizes-too-large sweats a look. "I know that you don't want anything sexy, but . . ."

I ram the clothes back in the oversized shopping bags they came in. "I hope you can get your money back."

"Sweetie, you need to get out more."

I rage at her. "I need *you* t*o* let *me* live *my* life."

"I made you an appointment."

"What?" Didn't she get it? My mother is so dense, she should rent herself out to a nuclear power plant as radiation shielding.

"Sweetie, the therapist said that you are young. Your brain could establish new pathways. You could regain control of your foot."

"And all I have to do is go through three more operations. Try to understand." I get in her face, two inches from her nose. I shout at her at full volume. "I've had enough pain! I can't take anymore! Get out! Get out!"

I grab her arm, drag her to the door, and throw her out of my apartment. *Slam.* The sound echoes in my brain. Slam: Forget about dating. I'm afraid of men. Slam: I'll never be able to live independently. I'm 28 years old and my mom still grocery shops for me because I'm afraid to leave my apartment. Slam: I'll never be able to teach again. I'm no good to anyone. I'm worthless.

I collapse onto the couch.

Jack, whimpering, hops up beside me.

"What did we do to deserve this? Do you hate God, too?"

He reaches out with his paw, touches me . . .

. . . and the world changes.

I yelp. Scents of grass and soil and wild jasmine growing on the dog park fence fill my nose. But as sweet as the jasmine is, there is something else, even sweeter, flitting through the bright sky with yellow wings. I run after it. I jump trying to fly with it. It darts a crazy path, rising, falling, now sideways. So quick! And with every flap of its wings, sweetness gushes into the air.

"Jack! Jack!" I turn at the sound of my own voice. Happiness fills me. I see me, my short, easy-to-fix, blond hair ruffled up by the breeze. The sun glints off it. With my fuzzy vision, it looks like a halo.

Wild anticipation courses through me. My feet won't be still. I jump. I run toward me, my eyes trying to focus on the whirling disc. Jack's joy becomes my own. He has no words, but I feel his emotions. *Throw it! Throw it! When is she going to throw it? Now? Are you going to throw it now? Yes!*

I run, following it with my eyes. Suddenly, it comes into sharp focus. It's falling . . . got it.

. . . and the world changes.

I'm splashing in water, wonderfully warm water. Yuck! It tastes awful. I slap my tail against it; flop into it. I see me again, wet hair clinging to my head. I lick my own face.

. . . and the world changes.

I am back on the couch with Jack beside me. The vision replays itself in my mind, especially the part where I'm chasing the butterfly and I hear my own voice calling out Jack's name. In the vision, I turn and see myself as Jack sees me. I look like an angel. Me, crippled and hopeless; I am Jack's angel.

Tears run down my face. I cradle Jack against my chest, rubbing my cheek against his fur.

"I'm nothing, boy. Don't you understand? I'm not worth you."

Jack

He yelps and licks my face.

I turn on the TV, but the shows come and go and still I'm sitting with this terrible awfulness inside. Beside me, Jack rolls on his back. I rub his tummy. The hair has grown back on his paw in a crooked line. "Guess you'll have that scar forever, boy."

Eventually, I turn off the TV, and Jack falls asleep. I stare at the blank screen. I pace, walking from room to room. I wipe up a drop of orange juice on the kitchen table, tie up the trash to take out tomorrow, water my cactus. The clock glows 10:13 p.m. I wake Jack.

"Boy, I need you to help me. Show me what I need to see. Please."

I look into his eyes, his wonderful soft brown eyes. I touch his paw,

. . . and the world changes.

Normal vision; must be my own past. My weak human nose tells me where I am—disinfectant. All hospitals smell the same.

Mom's diction is perfect. "Peter Piper picked a peck of pickled peppers."

I mumble, "Peerrr Piirr pe a pecc of pic—" The "l" in "pickled" is lost somewhere in my throat. I stop.

"Try it again, dear."

"Nnooo."

"Peter Piper picked a peck of pickled peppers."

Tears roll down my face. I scribble on a piece of paper, my handwriting only slightly better than my speech.

What's the use?

Sobs shake me. Mom takes my broken body into her arms. "I'm here, sweetie. I'm right beside you. I know, I understand. You've got to fight, baby. You've got to fight."

Fur, *Feathers,* and Scales

. . . and the world changes.

"Mom . . . oh, God, Mom."

My foot fails me, I fall. I crawl to my phone. Push favorites. Hers is the only number listed.

"Mom?" I sob out her name. "Mom, I'm sorry."

"No, sweetie, I understand. You want to live an independent life. You've lost so much. I'm a pest."

"No, Mom, that's not it. I don't need to be independent. I mean . . . I thought I did. But I realize now that what I need to be . . . is grateful. Yeah, I walk funny, but I've got you. All this time, I took you for granted. Oh, dear God, Mom, you fed me. You helped me go to the bathroom. You even slept beside me those first days in this apartment, when I was too scared to be alone. You were there for me. You held me. Mom, you taught me to talk again. I was so busy feeling sorry for myself and being afraid, that I never saw you."

"Sweetie, you don't have to thank me."

"Yes, I do. Mom, I need to thank you. And more than that, I *want* to thank you. Please, maybe tomorrow you could come back over? I'd like to try on those clothes. And Mom, if you'll help me, I'll have the surgeries."

"Sweetie, you don't have to."

"I know, but I've got this fantastic Mom. And with you, I can do anything. I love you, Mom."

I hear her weeping. *Uh-oh.* She's not good with emotion. Weeping? That's way too hard for her. I glance down at Jack and wink.

"So, Mom, here's the deal. I'm having a problem about going back to teaching. I mean . . . well, what if I fall down in class?"

Jack

"Oh," the crying abruptly stops. "We'll practice, sweetie. I'll come over tomorrow..."

Six Feet Under

Dianna Sinovic

The ants swarmed on the bedroom carpet, a churning black mass that spread toward the picture window. Those with wings flew a few feet, then dropped onto the comforter and pillows.

"Oh my god," Ned Thrips's wife shrieked. "Do something about them." She batted the flying ants away from her face and fled the room, still in her pajamas.

Ned disliked springtime because it brought the yearly influx of carpenter ants—and Marion's insistence that he get rid of them. He guessed that the swarm had reached capacity in some hidden area of the house, having feasted on the joists that held up the floors, and now were heading for fresh forests to fell. Uneasily, he wondered if one morning, as he rolled out of bed, the entire upper story might collapse from the concealed damage the ants had wrought.

He hated ants and every other kind of insect, and he blamed that squarely on Jesse Dodd. When they were both boys of seven, Jesse, his soon-to-be-ex-best-friend, put a June beetle down his back at recess. Ned yelled in fright, waving his arms and jumping up and down—while Jesse laughed. Ned was forever-after dubbed the chicken of the playground.

Fur, *Feathers*, and Scales

Everything about bugs creeped him out. Six legs, big abdomen—although his was plenty plump too—and antennae that waved around. What was not to dislike?

Ned's philosophy was murder on sight, whether by shoe or sandal or rolled-up Penny Power. Seeing a smashed carapace or mashed wings brought him much satisfaction. He secretly dreamed of buying a belt inscribed à la the Grimm fairy tale: *Seven in one swat!*

Or perhaps someday someone might dub him the Lord of the Flies.

Insects weren't all that Ned abhorred. He generously included spiders and millipedes, ticks and slugs in his panoply of pests to be gotten rid of. When his son, Hollis, pointed out that spiders were not insects and that slugs had no legs, Ned shrugged his shoulders. "They're all the same to me."

And wherever he turned, Ned seemed to run into the pests. Cockroaches at the gym, mosquitoes hovering near the hot tub, paper wasps in the pear tree—and there was Ned, quick on his feet, ready to mash them into insect pulp.

Of course, sometimes his foes fought back. One summer at high school band camp, he was marching across a fallow field with his fellow clarinetists, thoughts on the hot new color-guard member. Cassandra, wasn't it? His line in the formation trailed the flutes and piccolos, and in the humid afternoon, sweat dripped from his brows as he half-heartedly played "Hang On, Sloopy." Then he realized the formation was doing maneuvers he hadn't been told of, as students at the front began to pivot quickly and run for the sidelines. Had he missed a practice? Then, as the clarinets kept marching, Ned saw the reason for the fast change in lineup: a swarm of ground hornets. He grabbed his clarinet with one hand and his music in the other and ran with the rest to safety.

Six Feet Under

If summer was bee season in his youth, he found that other times of the year had their own chitinous challenges once he had a family. Fall brought the stink bugs that covered the window screens each September. Hollis and his sister, Elsy, made a competition, seeing who could flick the most bugs off the screens. Ned loathed the bugs. His usual MO of squashing the enemy had ended badly.

"Dad," Hollis explained, with the preternatural patience that only a fourteen-year-old can muster when he knows he's right, "why do you think they're called *stink* bugs?"

Winter's gauntlet presented Ned with camel crickets in the basement, their antennae a good six inches long.

"Dad!" Elsy would scream up the stairs, when she descended into the depths for a clean pair of jeans from the dryer. "It's the crickets! I'll be late for school!"

And Ned would arm himself with his Wolverines (Contractor model) and clump down the steps in them to rescue his daughter.

Ned forbade any pets in the family home. Hollis and Elsy cried at the edict, but Ned refused to back down. Dogs meant fleas and ticks and heartworms. Cats meant fleas and ticks and lice.

Then Marion begged for a parakeet. "I had a budgie growing up," she pleaded with him. "They're sweet birds that live in cages. You won't have to touch him—ever."

But all Ned could see were seed weevils and grain moths and red mites. "No," he said.

He finally wavered with the request for a fish tank. *What harm would that pose?* Hollis picked out the neon tetras, and Elsy chose the guppies and the mollies. It wasn't until he overheard Hollis talking to a friend that he discovered what else the tank was home to.

"My dad, well, he's an entomophobe," Hollis said, talking on his cell from the back porch, apparently unaware that Ned was standing just around the corner. "He's scared

Fur, *Feathers,* and Scales

of bugs. Okay, not *scared* of them, but he hates them, and other crawly things like spiders."

Ned nodded to himself. *Absolutely true.*

"He wouldn't let me or my sister have a dog or cat or other pet, because they might have bugs on them," Hollis continued. "But we do have fish, some really cool ones. But here's a secret."

Hollis paused, and Ned crept closer to the corner of the house.

"My dad doesn't know the fish tank also has these tiny worms that eat fish poop and these really tiny snails. He would probably freak out if he did."

Absolutely true, Ned thought. The fish tank didn't last more than a day after that fateful phone call.

The carpenter ants in the bedroom heralded a next step for Ned. He was tired of Marion's continued harping about the insects, and so vowed to exterminate them once and for all. No more rolled-up newspapers. He needed a better weapon.

After breakfast on that spring Saturday, Ned brought the vacuum cleaner up to the bedroom. He flexed his muscles, smiling to himself: He was Ant-Man reporting for pest control duty. Switching on the vacuum, he suctioned up all the ants he could see, even sucking some out of midair. Then he surveyed the battlefield. Not an ant in sight. It was gratifying to have won this first round, but he knew the enemy troops were massing beyond the walls.

For round two, he drove to the hardware store for more ammunition.

"What you need is a dusting powder to sprinkle around the room," the clerk advised. "That'll do it."

"No, no." A man standing in line just behind Ned spoke up. "Use boric acid mixed with sugar. Put that in little containers around the room. The ants will be attracted to it and keel right over."

Six Feet Under

Ned shook his head. "I need to stop these things right now. My wife is going bananas with them flying all around the bedroom." He didn't add: *And I'm not far behind her.*

He ended up with a pump sprayer and a general-purpose insecticide. The clerk argued that the dusting powder was safer, but Ned figured whatever spray he didn't use on the ants, he could aim at the paper wasps and garden slugs outdoors. He could morph from Ant-Man into the Green Hornet.

"Can I help, Dad?" Hollis tagged along behind Ned as he climbed the stairs to the master bedroom, armed with the sprayer.

Ned set the sprayer down in the bedroom doorway. "I appreciate the offer, son, but this stuff is bad for you. It's better for me to handle it myself."

"How long will the stuff take to work?"

Ned lifted the container of insecticide to read the label. "I'm not sure, but it will be quick. Your mother and I should be able to sleep in here tonight."

Once Hollis was headed back downstairs, Ned slipped on the special gloves the hardware clerk had insisted he buy and poured the chemical into the sprayer. The day was cool, with a fresh breeze, so he opened the bedroom windows wide to vent any noxious vapors once he started to work. Despite the draft, he was sweating slightly. He was nervous, but not sure why—these were ants, not tarantulas.

He pumped the sprayer to build up pressure, following the directions he'd seen on YouTube, then strapped the respirator—another must-have, the clerk said—over his nose and mouth.

With the sprayer tank in his left hand and the nozzle in his right, he worked his way around the baseboards, evenly coating the wood. He wasn't sure where the ants were coming from, but they had first appeared on the floor. After making a complete circuit of the room, he paused to decide what else to spray. The scent of the insecticide was mildly sweet, even through the mask.

Two ants crawled out of an electrical outlet, made their way down the wall to the baseboard, frantically waved their antennae, and fell to the floor.

"Gotcha," Ned said, pleased with his work. "Let me just take care of any of your buddies hiding in there. I'm getting rid of every last one of you, if it's the last thing I do." He knelt to better aim the nozzle into the outlet.

Marion found him later, when she went to find out why the breaker had blown. He was stretched out on the carpet, dead.

Cast Away in Seam Water

Paul Weidknecht

The ride to Gram's farm every May never failed to enchant Lily. Already thick and green, the grass combined with the explosion of flowering trees—dogwood in pink, crabapple in white—to send a salutation of color back into the land. Warm air whipped inside the car, carrying the cloyed fragrances of pollen and manure as they passed mile after mile of freshly turned slabs of wet soil ready for planting. All of it felt like an apt reward after a hard winter sealed inside their apartment in the city.

Each year her mom pulled them from school on Friday for a three-day vacation that Lily wished could last forever. The countryside was a departure from their regular lives, hers in middle school, Brent's in high school. Mom and Gram would relax on the porch and laugh about silly events from decades ago that only they understood, Brent would walk back to Gramp's workshop for the fishing gear—*There's only one May a year, and I'm going to spend it throwing flies to trout*—and Lily would take her current favorite book beneath that big magnolia in the side yard, letting her imagination wander, as usual. Yet, she knew, this year could never be like the past.

Lily glanced over at Mom from the passenger seat. She was crying quietly again, like everyone else over the past month, taking turns, purging themselves of the grief that kept refilling. Obviously, no one took it well, but her mother seemed nearest to the point of collapse.

"You know," her mother said in a half-cry, half-laugh, "Brent would be talking right now about some *bug* he was certain would be hatching this evening at Gram's stream."

"You're right. He'd tell us the Latin name of the such-and-such stonefly spinner thing."

"He was a real trout nerd."

"Geek, Mom. He would've liked that better. It's a little more updated."

Her mom reached over and gave her knee a shake, smiling through her tears. For the next several miles they said nothing.

"I want you to know, Lily, that I love you very much."

"And I love *you* very much."

"No, what I mean is that I'm telling you so we both remember this moment, driving here to Gram's, on this day. I don't remember saying that to Brent. I know I did, especially while he was in the hospital, but I just don't know of any other specific times."

"Of course you told him."

"But you can't recall a time in particular, and I can't either. And that's a terrible shame."

Acute lymphoblastic leukemia. Lily remembered the first time her mom said it; she had the doctor write it down on the back of his business card, had to sound it out like a child with a new spelling word. Brent had become pale, weak. Food didn't interest him anymore. Every time he bumped himself, no matter how lightly, he would bruise, anywhere, everywhere. They found out age sixteen put him squarely in the high-risk category. They would go on to hear about the science of immature white blood cells, the ecstasy of remission, and the horror of relapse.

Cast Away in Seam Water

It didn't help that her father decided two weeks after Brent's diagnosis he wasn't cut out for watching the chemo/radiation thing happen to his son; too depressing, he said; handholding was not his strong play, he explained. Within three weeks, he had moved a thousand miles away and started a home business from his new apartment, something he'd mentioned dreamily at the dinner table every so often. He showed up for the funeral and flew back out of town the same night.

"There's Gram," Lily said, as they pulled into the dirt driveway of the farm. "Waiting for us on the porch."

"Look at her face, Lily. So different from other years."

The farm no longer functioned as such and had not since Gramp's heart attack years ago. After he died, Gram leased out the land to neighboring farmers, keeping a small section for a garden, vegetables she'd sell along with her jellies and honey at the roadside stand out by the mailbox. The stand operated on an honor system: mark down on the yellow ledger tablet what you bought, leave your money in the cashbox, make change if you need to; that is, until last summer, when someone drove away with the cashbox and a half-dozen ears of corn. Now, if a car pulled up, Gram would wander onto the porch and wave.

Gram gave her mom a tight hug and opened an arm to draw Lily into their embrace. She felt Gram's muscles collect her in, possessing a warmth that came from a deep mutual loss. After their greeting, they carried in the luggage, with Lily walking upstairs to the bedroom she used every year. When she returned downstairs, instead of heading to the magnolia with her book, she walked to Gramp's workshop.

She leaned in, staring through the windowed door, her hands cupped around her eyes. Fishing and tools never interested her, so she never found herself inside the workshop; in fact, when she was younger, the place felt vaguely scary. Lily turned the wobbly doorknob and slowly stepped

Fur, *Feathers*, and Scales

beyond the wooden threshold splintered concave from Gramp and his father. The air was stale, musty from old wood and time. Metal signs advertising chewing tobacco, soda, and cigars filmed in dust hung from hooks screwed into the ceiling beams. Ball jars of nails, nuts, and bolts sat in rows on shelves above the sawdust-flecked worktable, and spider webs rounded the corners of the windows. A desk and rolling chair sat on the far side of the shop, where a small towel was draped over some unseen object, reminding her of a miniature statue before its unveiling. Gramp's three fly rods lay on finely sanded and varnished wooden braces on the wall. Above the rods hung a colorful poster showing the illustration of a fish with a brilliant orange belly and tiny red dots haloed in light blue, labeled in block letters: BROOK TROUT. It appeared newer than the other items, probably something Brent had put up. She walked across the cement floor to the desk.

Lily lifted the towel. From watching Brent a few times, she recognized the object as a tying vise. She pulled out the chair, sat, and slid open the center drawer, the release of air sending several strands of black marabou floating upward like wisps of smoke. Feathers, spools of thread, boxes of hooks, patches of fur, and some strange-looking tools she didn't recognize crowded this drawer. The other drawers contained what had to be every single item a person would need for fly-fishing: reels, green line, yellow line, flies, fly boxes, books on tying, books on casting, books on insects, a journal, more feathers, glue, gold beads, a thermometer (?), a tiny turkey baster thing (??), stuff to make a fly float, stuff to make a fly sink, stuff.

Kicked back in the chair with her hands behind her head, Lily found herself curious about the rods on the wall. They looked way too thin and frail to bring in any fish. She realized dinner wouldn't be ready for hours, more than enough time to continue exploring.

Cast Away in Seam Water

Lily wasn't sure if it was the smell of bacon or the morning sunlight that woke her, but the new day had arrived and already she had a story to tell.

Bounding down the stairs, Lily began her revelation.

"Mom, I have to tell you something!"

She heard nothing.

"Lily," Gram called out.

Reaching the bottom of the stairs into the kitchen, she cut toward the porch. Gram gently corralled her.

"Honey," she said softly, "your mother's out on the porch. She's having a rough time today. She needs to hear something good."

Lily nodded solemnly and dipped her head through the doorway. Her mother sat slouched in the porch swing, holding a cup of tea, staring out over the fields across the road. She lazily turned her head, smiling weakly, her eyes limp. She looked exactly as she had described herself several times over the last month: hollowed-out.

"Hi, sweetie."

"Hi, Mom."

"Sleep well?"

"Yeah. How about you?"

"I'll give it another try tonight. I hope you're hungry. Gram has one of her famous breakfasts going on in there. By the way, what did you want to tell me?"

"I know this is going to sound really weird, but just listen. Last night I had a dream. One of those lucid dreams, you know, the kind where you know it's a message rather than one of those crazy dreams that jumps around and makes no sense. Anyway, I saw Brent."

Her mother stared at her for a moment before placing the teacup on the side table next to her.

Fur, *Feathers,* and Scales

"The whole scene was misty, like I was watching through a very sheer curtain. I saw him standing in this meadow, on the opposite side of this amazing, crystal-clear stream. He was smiling, then he waved. He was so happy."

"Honey."

"Then suddenly I'm sitting at a table with two flies in front of me, but they're not small, they're giant-sized, like maybe as big as my laptop screen, so I can see every detail. Just then Brent's hand comes into my side vision—I know it's his hand because of the scar on the knuckle from when he cut himself whittling—and points at the flies one at a time, like he's teaching, like he's telling us what will work."

"Lily, this isn't—"

"And I believe the two flies match the remaining two days we'll be here, so—"

"No, okay, stop."

"Mom, Brent wants us to go fly-fishing."

Her mother became silent, and her lips parted as if she was halfway between wondering about a thought and speaking it, and this thought was now spiraling into some place of insight and understanding. Then reality seemed to call.

"Lily, we don't know anything about fly-fishing."

"Come on, Mom. We'll figure it out. How tough can it be?"

Gram admitted that she didn't know as much about their stream as Gramp, but that he said it was a spring creek, stayed pretty much the same temperature in winter or summer. He told her that it held only brown trout, and that they weren't easy to catch. She remembered him saying once that grasshopper flies worked well in August; but it wasn't August.

Cast Away in Seam Water

Lily considered this as she and Mom walked down the back stoop toward the field. A line of trees several hundred yards away marked the location of the creek. They passed the pair of pale, domeless silos encased in dry, dark vines, the crumbling stone springhouse, with its slates tilted and sliding. Lily carried the single rod they would share, the one she thought Brent had used during previous visits; she figured they could use any luck available.

"Now, I don't know much about casting," Lily said, "but getting the fly out there has to do with the weight of the line and the action of the rod. The fly we're using today is called a Royal Coachman. It has a red middle, with sparkly green stuff on the ends."

"Where did you get all this from?"

"Well, you know, the dream. At least the fly description, anyway. I remembered what it looked like, went online, and found the name."

Her mother looked over and grinned. "Okay."

"When I was about your age," her mom continued, "I would go back to the creek to relax. I never fished, but occasionally, I'd sneak up and watch the trout. More often than not, they'd see me or my shadow and be gone, but if I kept low, I could watch them. Sitting in the current, holding between the fast and slow water, they emitted a grace by just being natural, by just being themselves. And they didn't even know it."

Five minutes later they arrived at the tree line and low stone wall marking the end of the property. They stood in the shade for a moment, cool and hidden. The creek did not babble, but flowed quietly, with no boulders to go over, few fallen trees to go around. They were treated to the aquarium-like view of cream and tan-colored pebbles speckling the streambed, patches of underwater vegetation undulating with the current. A small brown trout hovered, its dark shadow more visible against the bed than its body. It shot to the surface, pocking the water.

"Did you see that?" her mom asked.

"Yes," Lily whispered. "We have to find a way to get to that fish. You know the saying: Always cast to a rising fish."

"Where did you hear that?"

"The dream. Plus, it's sort of common sense. But we can't cast from these trees."

Her mother made a face. "Lily, we can't cast, period."

"True."

Lily scanned for an opening to come out ahead of the trout. She motioned to her mother, and they walked upstream. They emerged from the shade into the sunlight. Lily stripped out the fly line, the coiled leader, her best-guess knot, and the Coachman. She swung the rod, the fly landing in the water five feet from her. The fly began to pull slowly toward the middle of the flow. As the fly reached the trout, she braced herself. The trout stirred from its lane, nosed up to the colorful fly, and quickly dipped away.

"Oh, I thought that was it," her mother said.

"That trout looked scared of the fly," Lily said. "Or insulted by it."

That fish never came to hand, nor did any others. After three hours of walking and fishing the creek in the brightness of a high sun, Lily and Mom decided to go back, tired and discouraged. They had come to the realization that while intelligence might not be the most notable characteristic of trout, pickiness can be a good camouflage for it, and the result is identical. They also discovered that in order to have a frontcast, there must be a backcast, and that tree branches and flies are magnetic.

"Maybe we started too early," Lily offered. "We should've gotten here a little later, more toward the time when they eat."

"It seems they eat about the time we eat."

Cast Away in Seam Water

"We can have a late supper tomorrow. Gram will understand," Lily said without looking up. "Tomorrow'll be better."

A chilled breeze blew from west to east, pushing heavy gray clouds across the sky. The pall stretched over the meadow, shrouding the passive evening light, as the tall grass bobbed in the wind. The two stared into the creek; no aquarium today. In fact, had they not seen fish yesterday, they would have wondered if the creek held trout at all.

"Hon," her mother said. "If we see lightning, we're leaving. I don't want us getting caught crossing this field in a storm."

Lily nodded as she took out more line, now faster. "This is the second fly Brent showed me: the Elk Hair Caddis. It's a bristly tan fly that doesn't look anything like what we used yesterday."

She cast the fly and let it drift until the line was straight. Nothing. She continued the process—only guessing it was correct—and still there were no rises. Even genuine insects floated down the creek until they were out of sight, all of their journeys uninterrupted. Cast after cast for the next fifteen minutes yielded nothing. The wind picked up, and Lily felt a small sense of unease ripple through her.

A tiny fork of lightning flashed on the western horizon. She cast quickly, hoping her mother had missed it.

"Lily."

"That wasn't lightning."

"We should probably start wrapping it up."

Lily put the fly in again. She wanted one of these brown trout; for Mom, for herself, for Brent. She knew the second she told her mother the story about the dream that catching a fish was a big part of it. They needed to do this, together.

Her mother cleared her throat before she spoke:

"*Troth's Tan Elk Hair Caddis has to be one of the best all-around flies ever. Good visibility, great floatability. Can be used as a caddis imitation when naturals are present, also as a searching pattern. Size 14 works well, but try a sparse-tie 16 if the 14 is not working. Caught two small browns.*'"

Lily froze. The rod tip faded toward the water, and she gradually turned around.

"You're not mad at me, Mom, are you?"

Her mom closed the journal. "I could never be mad at you, Lily. It doesn't matter how he reached us—by dream or journal—he still reached us."

"I'm sorry. I didn't mean to lie or anything like—"

"Don't apologize for love. By the way, you got all this information from Brent's journal?"

"Mostly. The internet helped a little, too."

"But we do have a problem, Lily."

"What's that?"

"We have to hope there's a sparse-tie 16 in that fly box. Is 16 bigger or smaller?"

"Smaller, even though the number is bigger. It's one of those weird fly-fishing things."

Lily opened the fly box, looking for the gap that had held the size 14 Elk Hair Caddis. Next to it had to be the size 16. She plucked a smaller version of that fly from the foam, then snipped off the size 14 and replaced it with the 16.

"It doesn't have much elk hair on it, or that body stuff, but, here." Lily said, handing the rod to her mother. Lightning flashed again, followed by a boom of thunder that made them jump.

"No, Lily, you should."

Lily shook her head. "Mom, that's your fish in there."

Her mother took the rod in one hand, the spooled-out line in the other.

Cast Away in Seam Water

"Remember, Mom, a frontcast needs a backcast."

Her mother brought back the rod, the fly line whipping up from the grass. When the line was straight out behind her, she drove it forward with her wrist.

An odd gust of wind carried the line, leader, and fly to the center of the creek. The fly bumped softly on top of the water, swirled when it hit the seam, and was eaten.

Her mother gasped and twitched the rod. The fish thrashed at the surface, once, twice, then drew the line in a half-circle, before digging for the opposite bank.

"Mom, don't let it get near that log."

Her mother raised the rod tip, and the fish curved back toward their bank. It splashed on the surface three or four more times, turned toward them, then rested on its tether, already seemingly needing a breather. Her mother kneeled and guided the fish—perhaps six inches long—toward her submerged hand. She lifted her hand, and the fish lay in her palm. Lily leaned over her mom's shoulder.

Her mother examined the fish closely. "Lily, look at the colors on that little guy. The orange belly, those tiny red dots, the blue around them."

Lily leaned in and shook her head. "I think that's a brook trout. Weren't there only supposed to be brown trout in here? It doesn't belong."

"No, Lily, it belongs, and I have a feeling I know how it got here."

When I Was Your Age

Marianne H. Donley

"When I was *your* age, I had to walk five miles through the snow to get to school. And I never complained," bleated Old Goat to his kid Billy on the first day of middle school.

"Gosh, Dad, I didn't know it snowed in Hawaii," Billy said. "And I'm not complaining."

"Go clean your room."

Some years later, Billy's kid brother Bobby started middle school.

"When I was your age," Old Goat snorted, "I had to walk ten miles through the snow, without a coat, to get to school. And I never complained."

"Gee, Dad, I'm not complaining," little Bobby said. "But I thought Grandma said you rode your bike."

"Go weed the garden."

Fur, *Feathers,* and Scales

Finally, baby Barry Goat was old enough for middle school.

"When I was your age, I had to walk twenty miles uphill through the snow without a coat and without shoes to get to school," grunted Old Goat, "and I never complained."

"Golly, Dad, who's complaining," said Barry Goat. "Grandpa was the school bus driver. Why didn't you ride with him?"

"Go sweep the patio."

Moral: The distance an old goat walked to school is always directly proportional to his age.

CRITTER

Diane Sismour

The equestrians file out from the warm barn into the brisk December air. Small bursts of hot breath puff from the horses' nostrils on their way into the stable yard. The sky is gray, and the weatherman promises snow to fall in a few hours. The riders are wearing riding helmets, trim riding pants, and bright quilted vests, adding colorful splashes to the bleak Pennsylvania landscape.

I collect their lesson fees and check the chin straps on each helmet and the cinch girth of every saddle before the six kids can mount up for their English Equitation lesson. "Chrissie, Mom said to tell you she'll write a check after the lesson," says the last student before she climbs astride.

This is the second time this month her parent has forgotten to pay me! *I'll have to speak with her mother soon before this becomes a habit*, I think, and walk ahead to open the indoor arena's gate.

My gloved fingers straighten the bills. Most 16-year-olds save to buy a car, but not me. Soon I'll have enough money to buy my very own horse. I shove the crisp cash into the pocket of my heavy barn coat. There's no time for dreaming today . . . not with a storm brewing.

The riders bend figure-eight turns and practice gait changes to prepare their mounts. The horses sense that a storm is coming, too; their steps are springy and tails arch high in excitement.

"Keep a hold on them," I say. "You're in for some spunky rides today."

Before the hour-long lesson ends, snowflakes drift in through the arena's sliding door. Parents line the gate, hurrying us along. The snow is falling in steady, small flakes. This kind of storm can dump a foot or more before the day is over. With fifteen minutes remaining, ending early is the right call.

"Dismount and lead your horses to the barn. Unsaddle and I'll groom your mounts."

Parents and students scurry to the tack room to hang saddles and bridles.

I hear Dad's dual-wheel pickup truck rumble up the stone driveway and watch him skirt the edge as the cars race past him. He parks alongside the paddock and ambles into the barn with a large sack of oats over his shoulder.

I open the feed bin, and he dumps it into the wooden box. "I have good news. . . . I saw Molly at the feed mill, and she has a filly to show you," he says. He looks out into the storm. "We can go look at her tomorrow. It'll be a slow day here."

Molly has pointed out two other horses that didn't fit into my meager six-hundred-dollar budget. They were both older and already partially broke to ride. I'm looking for a horse to train that can become a champion someday, to make an investment in my own equestrian career.

The next day we follow a plow truck the entire mile drive to Molly's farm and lean against the fence railing to watch a dun-colored Appaloosa filly play in the field. Her coat is the color of funnel cake with a sprinkling of powdered sugar over her hips. The snow bounces off her hooves as she trots down the pasture path effortlessly. I'm picturing her flaxen mane and tail flowing in the breeze, when, in reality, she's a mess, with burrs snarled in her coat and tail.

The young mare tosses her nose at us. I say, "She's beautiful, Dad. Don't you think?"

Dad pushes up the bill of his Phillies baseball cap. "You know she can't come on the road with us. You won't have much time to train her."

Her ears pin back, and I watch her chase another horse away from the hay trough. "She is a wild one."

The other horses put more distance between them and her. There is just something captivating me about the horse that I can't quite place. The glint in her eye should be enough to warn me, but I'm a girl in love.

"I think she's the one."

He shakes his head. "It's your money, your decision," he says, but his smile is a dead giveaway. He sees her potential, too.

Molly coaxes the filly into the barn with grain and backs out of the stall, closing the door behind her slowly. "We just found her last weekend at the auction, and she looked like one that might interest you."

As I open the thick wooden door to enter, the filly lashes out with a hoof to keep me from approaching. "Aren't you a sweetheart?" I mock.

She spins and lands a kick on my thigh in answer.

The heavy layers of winter clothing add some protective padding against the blow, but—*ouch!* That hurt. The horse is not to blame, since I invaded her space, but her sharp hoof is still going to leave a deep bruise.

"You are an ornery critter." Her ears swivel to listen as she moves away from me deep into the far corner. The filly's new nickname speaks volumes about her. Critter fits her personality perfectly. My inner voice is shouting at me to stop . . . that I will regret this action later, but I see a challenge worth the pain of dealing with the nastiness and negotiate a deal.

The next morning, Dad and I remove a partition from the trailer and return. We back up to the stall door entrance. The greedy mare smells the sweet alfalfa hay and can't resist temptation. She hops into the trailer. By the time we drive the short distance home, she has finished all but a few bites. As soon as the tailgate swings open, Critter tosses her nose and stomps her hooves as she trots around her new home in the paddock.

Usually a foal's handling begins at birth, and they are halter-broke to lead when only a few weeks old because of their manageable size. On January first, Critter officially turns two years old, and this 700-pound horse never wore a halter before. Dad lassoes the mare to gain control and loops the rope around her nose to use as a temporary halter until we can get close enough to fit her with a proper one.

Training the mare to lead confirms her stubbornness. My inner voice was right, but I'm stubborn, too. Hearing "I told you so" this early into her training just won't do.

It takes one of us to tug the rope, and the other with a comealong tied behind her, to gain the first stiff-legged steps. When the rope slides too high along her flanks, she bolts forward, dragging me behind her. We progress literally one step at a time. The certainty I have of turning this ratty-looking horse into what I envision is slipping away with each new bruise she gives me.

Critter learns trust in small doses. After some horrific days of struggling, she stands tied without pulling backward and learns that once the halter is off, she is free again. Exercising on the long line turns to free lunging, and I use voice commands to control the pace by singing different songs. She must consider the reward of moving without restraints a victory, because our relationship is a constant

CRITTER

battle. There are more days I regret every dime spent on her than not.

Although I'm only able to work with her between competitions, the strides Critter makes in six months moves her training beyond the other two-year-olds. She gains more height and muscle with regular workouts. By late summer, she is fit to saddle, another adventure unto itself.

No horse I ever rode acted so obstinate, and she takes longer to break than most because of it. Critter turns left when signaling right, runs through the bit instead of stopping, and stands as a mule when asked to move. The mare is enjoying a good battle of wits, and figuring out how to outmaneuver her becomes a lesson in wills between us. One of us is going to be sway, and it isn't going to be me.

We select Critter and two other three-year-old fillies to ride in the winter circuit, where they'll learn the crash course in show-ring etiquette at the winter riding events. I'm more than a little nervous. The host stable doesn't have the easiest arena to teach a young horse the ropes. There is competition in an arena filled with horse trainers out to pursue the same advantage: to season their green horses amid the noise and confusion found at a show ring before the regular season begins six weeks later.

I rode Alibi, a well-behaved stallion, in the Western and English pleasure classes the previous year. He nearly jumped out of his horseshoes when the loudspeaker screeched and the indoor arena walls rattled as the winter wind blasted in from the west. If Alibi reacted so poorly, I can only guess how Critter will act.

Grooming shaggy hair increases Critter's education in standing patiently. She is still quick to lash out. The first few times the farrier shod her, we lifted a second foot on the diagonal to protect him from undue harm. However, there is no one else at the barn tonight, and I am on my own.

Fur, *Feathers,* and Scales

The horse clippers rattle in my hand as I trim her fetlocks, and all my senses are alert for any threat. Forty-five minutes into grooming her, I squat beside the rear leg and relax after managing the first three without any mishaps. A big mistake; she feigns a kick, I fall backward, and the mare slams down on my foot.

"Get off me." No amount of pushing from that low angle removes the weight off my boot, and I jab her in the flank with the clippers. The vibration jolts her forward, but the clippers cut a broad swatch of hair off her flank.

"Oh, crud." It is impossible to feather smooth a shaggy winter coat. I grit my teeth and resign myself to several more hours of clipping the hair on her entire body short to cover up my mistake. "Behave or I'll give you a poodle cut."

Early the next morning, Dad and I load the chosen mounts into the trailer and drive to the event at sunrise. When we arrive, I notice all the usual trainers attempting to tire their horses by working them in the outdoor warm-up arena, and know that no matter how long I attempt to wear her down, it is an exercise in futility. This January is no different from any other: the wind is blowing, and the metal walls will rattle. What little mental calm the mare has gained is certain to evaporate as soon as we unload her.

An hour later, the loudspeaker squawks for us to gather at the gate. The previous class is receiving their awards as we enter the ring. The ringmaster checks our contestant numbers as we enter, while handing ribbons to the winners as they exit the indoor arena. The ribbons' fluttering scares Critter, and she veers sideways, banging into another horse.

I nod an apology, but every trainer is expecting a few calamities in the ring at the first of the six-show series. "Welcome to the world of the winter show circuit," I mutter to Critter and pat her neck reassuringly. *If this training didn't create such tolerant animals for the regular season, nothing could drag me here . . . ever.*

Critter

The announcer calls all contestants to jog, and the class begins. Critter's ears pin back at every horse riding beside us, her strides lengthen, and we're stuck three-deep on the rail with nowhere to maneuver. The mare's body tenses, building up to lash out at whichever unfortunate competitor passes too close. I sing anything that comes to mind in a soft melodic tone. Her ears flick around to listen. My voice is soothing, and she falls into the rhythm, relaxing back into a slower step.

The judge is watching along a fence section at the opposite end of the arena, and we circle around to find a clear spot to ride a clean pass before him. Critter calms further in less traffic. Her ears point forward, we come to an opening, and I exhale knowing this pass in front of the judge is a winner.

Just as we are about to pass into the judge's view, a spectator beside us flails her arms overhead and screams at someone across the ring, "Circle, Sally, circle." Critter spooks, lunging forward, and bounces off the horse in front of us, setting off a domino of show-ring catastrophes. All around the arena riders are reining in their mounts for control.

Even though I have a lot of apologizing to do after this class, I am smiling. It was fleeting, but right before Critter skittered and caused the chaos, the image of the scruffy dun filly having the potential to become a champion changed to a reality. We have more work to do, but my intuition will pay off. *I just know it.*

Buttons

Ralph Hieb

When Jonathan Devonston returned home from work, he found both his wife, Irene, and their six-year-old daughter, Sarah, sobbing in each other's arms.

"What's wrong?" he asked. "Has something happened?"

Sniveling, his wife pointed to the back porch.

Walking out the back door and onto the porch, Jonathan saw Buttons, their dog, lying in the middle of the porch. In the afternoon sun, he was curled up as if sleeping, but Buttons wasn't moving.

"Oh, Buttons," Jonathan said, walking over to him and bending down to pat his head. "Well, old boy. It looks like you've had your last day playing. Now it's time to sleep."

Jonathan took off his suit jacket and spread it gently over the deceased animal. "I'll see about a good place to let you rest in peace."

Standing, collecting his emotions, and straightening his vest, he went back into the house.

Turning to his wife, Jonathan said, "I will leave Buttons on the porch for a bit. I must change if I am to dig his grave."

"Where will you put him?" Irene asked.

"Sarah," Jonathan said, looking at his daughter. "Is there any place you think Buttons would like to be laid to rest?"

With swollen eyes, Sarah looked at her father, then pointed to the back yard.

"Do you mean the space between the maple trees with the sun shining on it," her mother asked.

The child nodded.

"That will be a wonderful place. With this warm summer sun shining down on him. He will love it," Irene said. Then looking at Jonathan with pleading eyes, and holding their daughter, she mouthed the words, "What do we do?"

Jonathan knelt down, so he was at eye level with Sarah. "I'm going to see a friend of mine. And I'm going to ask him to find another dog just like Buttons. Would you like that?"

Sarah nodded. "Will he look like Buttons?" she asked quietly.

"Of course. Father will make sure that he does," Irene said in a soft voice, looking directly at Jonathan and still hugging her daughter.

Later that night, after Sarah had gone to bed, Irene said, "Now we've done it. How will we ever find a dog that looks like Buttons?" Irene poured two cups of tea. "When we got him, he was already old and starting to turn gray."

"I know. His age was a key factor in your sister giving him to us. As for what I intend to do, I'm going to ask Mr. Timmons if he can help."

"But he works for the Ministry of Metals. I don't see how that will help with our current problem," Irene said.

Buttons

"He is an expert tinkerer. I'm hoping that he will be able to build a replica of Buttons that uses some small steam engines."

"Do they make them that small?" she asked.

"You would be surprised at the minute sizes that come into the Ministry of Patents every week. I am sure that I can find one small enough to do what we need. Then all we need is for Mr. Timmons to build the dog and integrate one of the new electrical brains inside it."

"Do you think it will actually work?" Irene asked.

"You didn't believe me when I said that there is a machine that can fly. Now dirigibles are the most efficient way to travel between cities." Jonathan leaned back in his chair and relit a cigar that was sitting in a nearby ashtray.

Taking a sip of his tea, Jonathan added, "Of course, steam is the newest thing. Why, at the club, the members say that by the 1890s, everything will be powered by steam. Even carriages will become horseless. And from what I can gather, those electrical brains are a marvel. You can tell them precisely what you wish them to do, and they will obey. I will ask if one can be installed in the mechanical." Then, looking out of the kitchen window, he added. "I hope that Sarah will accept a mechanical replica."

"I hope so, too," Irene said.

Irene waved her hand in front of her face to dissipate the smoke. "Then ask Mr. Timmons to start as soon as is convenient. Any idea what he will charge for the project?" she added.

"I do not think much. He owes me several favors," Jonathan replied.

Two weeks later, Sarah was in her room and heard the sound of the front door opening, then closing.

Fur, *Feathers*, and Scales

"Sarah, come see what Father has for you," Irene called from the bottom of the stairway.

Downstairs, Sarah went into the parlor. Jonathan stood next the fireplace with a small bundle of fur in his arms.

"Buttons!" the child yelled, running to her father. Sarah picked up the dog and cuddled it. "I'm going to love you forever," she said. "He is now such a pretty puppy, and he looks just like my poor old Buttons did." Nearly out of breath, she added, "Can I keep him?"

"Father brought him home for you," Irene replied.

Still holding the small puppy, Sarah ran outside and sat on her swing. Her parents followed her.

"He's so cute and cuddly," Sarah exclaimed.

"Why don't you play fetch with him?" Irene asked.

"Can I?" Sarah asked.

"Of course," Jonathan answered. "He can do anything Buttons could do. And he will become a wonderful friend."

Setting the puppy down, Sarah picked up a stick and threw it. The puppy made yipping sounds as it ran to fetch the stick.

"Can I call him Buttons?" Sarah asked.

"Well, that is a fine name for him," Jonathan answered.

Irene smiled. "Sarah looks so happy again."

"And the best thing is that we will not have to housebreak him, and it should not take much to feed." Jonathan mumbled. "Very inexpensive."

While watching his daughter, Jonathan said, "Just some daily coal and water. Maybe once a day, dry his ears, as that is where the steam exits." At Irene's questioning look, he added, "The ash will exit as it would with a normal dog, so we just need to tell it to go outside when the internal ash container needs to be emptied."

"Perhaps I should place a bowl of coal bits and a dish of water for him on the back porch," Irene said. "And place an old newspaper for him to use." She chuckled. "I do not wish for paw prints or ash piles in the house when it is raining."

"A most excellent idea."

Sarah went running around the yard, holding a stick out to her side. "Come on, Buttons," she yelled, as the puppy bounded after her.

Sarah's parents watched her and Buttons play fetch and other games, before retiring to the house.

Irene was sitting, enjoying some tea with Jonathan. "She loves this Buttons so much. I can't believe that she doesn't even consider that he is a mechanical creature."

"Perhaps I should ask Mr. Timmons if he can make Buttons grow larger as time passes," Jonathan said.

"That would be a wonderful thing. Then Buttons can grow as Sarah does."

Putting her teacup down, Irene stood and watched Sarah through the dining room window. "I could watch those two play all day."

"My only request is that she does not neglect her lessons, and that she learns the proper maintenance of Buttons." Jonathan picked up his cup and took a sip. "You know how she gets involved in her activities and forgets her studies and responsibilities. However, right now, I am happy she is enjoying her new pet."

"I still cannot believe it," Irene said, while she straightened her skirt.

"Cannot believe what?" Jonathan asked, as he lit his cigar.

"It has been twelve years since you brought the mechanical Buttons home. And Sarah still plays with him every day. She has never grown tired of him."

Fur, *Feathers,* and Scales

"I would have believed her thoughts would have turned toward finding a suitable young man with which to raise a family by now," Jonathan said.

"Not all girls wish to be married by their eighteenth birthday," Irene replied. "Look, she still laughs when Buttons crunches down on his coal food and sticks his muzzle in the water bowl to suck the water up through his nose."

Jonathan shook his head. "She is just a young woman with childish likes." He lit a cigar, then settled in his favorite chair and opened the evening newspaper.

"You arranged for Mr. Timmons to update it every year. Why, it even understands complete sentences." Irene said. She hesitated, then added, "I am beginning to worry that she will only really love that mechanical instead of finding a suitable partner."

"I know. I am as much to blame as anyone for her desire to learn the workings of mechanicals." Jonathan gave an exasperated grunt and put down his newspaper. "But I wish she would be more like the daughters of my coworkers. You know, worried about the latest fashion, the best shops, the next party, friends."

"Precisely." Irene said, then added, "Instead, she spends time in the kitchen and bothers Cook about how to make dinner. Plus, she can build mechanicals with the best of tinkerers. And for a young lady, her room looks like a workshop, with all of those metal gears and whatnots lying around."

"Well, she knows more of electrical brains than any inventor I have met," Jonathan said.

"I do agree with you about that. I went into her room the other day, and she was reading how to improve the electrical brains. Can you imagine?" Irene said, irritated. "You are the one who insisted that she learn how to maintain Buttons. She might as well have been born a boy." Irene threw up her hands in frustration.

Buttons

Walking to the backyard door, Irene called out. "Sarah, time to get ready."

"Mother, do I have to go to the ball? I really do not wish to attend," Sarah complained.

"We received an invitation that included you," Irene said.

"Plus," Jonathan broke into the conversation, "all the eligible young women will be attending, looking their best. And my daughter will be amongst them. Who knows, you might even meet a young man to your liking."

"Very well." Sarah started walking toward the door. "Come along, Buttons. I suppose you will have to stay home and watch the house while we are gone."

A knock at the front door had one of the maids scramble to answer, but Irene was there first.

"Why, Mr. Harbor, it is so nice to see you," Irene said. "Please, come in. If you could wait in the parlor, Sarah should be down momentarily."

"Thank you, Mrs. Devonston," Mr. Harbor answered. "Please call me George."

Walking into the parlor, George looked around, wondering if young Miss Sarah Devonston would look as radiant as she did a fortnight ago at the ball. She had worn a beautiful cream and lavender ensemble that accented her auburn locks. Even though she was tall, she still only came as high as his shoulder, an excellent height for a wife, he thought.

"You look absolutely beautiful," George said as Sarah walked into the parlor, followed by a dog. The dog caused George to take a step back. "He is not vicious, is he?"

"No," Sarah answered. "Not at all." She petted the beast on the head, then said, "Mr. George Harbor, this is But-

Fur, *Feathers,* and Scales

tons. Buttons, this is my escort for this evening, Mr. George Harbor."

Buttons sat and raised his paw to shake with George. Hesitating, George said, "My word, he is well trained, and quite large." Then he bent slightly at the waist to also pet Buttons. "He is wonderfully behaved."

"Yes, thank you," Sarah laughed. "He would never attack anyone without my direct order."

She turned and indicated the maid who stood a few steps behind her. "Mr. Harbor, please meet Alice, who will be our chaperone this evening."

The maid gave a quick curtsey. "Pleased to meet you, sir."

As the two young people left the house with Alice following behind, Buttons curled up in front of the fireplace.

"Well, Irene," said Jonathan, "I think this is a fine evening, and I feel a leisurely stroll would do us both good." He offered her his hand. "We have given almost all of the staff their half-day, so let us enjoy the night air also. Maybe see if there are any spare tickets to the theater to be had."

"I agree," his wife answered. "Plus, Sarah is away and properly chaperoned. And we seldom have time for ourselves." She took his hand and smiled. "Just let me get my shawl."

As the couple left the house, a person in the shadows watched with anticipation. *I think this will be a wonderful payday.*

Looking around carefully, the man kept to the bushes and made his way to the rear porch. *What is the easiest way to enter?* he thought as he slowly examined the windows and door for access. *I need to use proper tools to leave as little evidence as possible. I'll return later with my tools.*

Buttons sat up, as if hearing something, and looked around the house before settling down in front of the fire-

Buttons

place once more. Sarah's earlier command to stay there made him return to his resting position.

"Miss Devonston, I believe it looks as though it might rain. Can I interest you in some tea at the tea parlor on the corner?" George asked.

"No, thank you." Sarah adjusted the shawl slightly higher on her shoulders. "I believe my parents would expect me to come straight home since the weather is taking a disagreeable turn."

"Very well. I shall see you to your door," George said.

They walked to Sarah's home, where George held the door for the women to escape the drizzling rain.

"Hello, Mother, Father," Sarah called out as she entered the home. "I have asked Mr. Harbor in for some tea." She paused. "That is quite strange. I believe there is no one at home other than us three."

"Even with a chaperone, I do not believe it is acceptable for me to remain in the house without at least one of your parents in attendance," George said. "Will I be able to call on you at some future date?"

"Definitely," Sarah said. "I will walk you to the door."

After Sarah saw George out, Alice approached her.

"Pardon, Miss." Alice said. "I better bring in the wash before it gets soaked."

"Of course, Alice. I shall put on water for some tea to help drive out the chill in the air."

Sarah walked past the parlor, and Buttons sat up.

"It is all right, Buttons." Sarah stopped and smiled at the dog. "Just lie there. I will call if I need you." Uneasy, the mechanical lay down again.

As Alice walked outside, she didn't notice the rear door was unlocked. She started to take laundry down from the clothesline, and the thief spotted her as he was about to enter the house.

Thinking the maid was alone and guessing no further help would be coming from inside, the thief tried to sneak into the house.

Hearing unknown footsteps, Buttons stood and followed the sound. Waiting at the kitchen door, he watched the thief. And waited for Sarah's command.

Spying Sarah, the thief decided that he would render her unconscious to make his escape easier, and if the maid came in to early, it would be her bad luck.

Approaching Sarah from the back, the thief made a noise, causing Sarah turned around.

"Who are you?" she demanded.

"No problems from you now, little girl." The thief held a police baton he had stolen from another of the homes earlier that day.

He swung, and Sarah stepped back, avoiding the weapon.

"Then we'll do this the hard way." He pulled a knife from his back pocket.

"Buttons, come here," Sarah yelled, her eyes staring at the blade.

"Who's Buttons?" the thief asked as he walked closer to Sarah.

"My dog."

"So, you have a little doggy with a cute little name," he said waving the knife in front of her face, smiling all the time.

He stopped as he heard a growl from behind him. Buttons had entered.

"I suggest you put down your knife." Sarah said. "Buttons would not like it if you tried to harm me."

Turning around he gasped. "What the . . ."

Buttons

"Buttons is extremely large for a King Sheppard." Sarah said, "And they are not a small breed to begin with."

A large, long-haired dog stared at the thief. It pulled back its lips, fully exposing long, sharp teeth. He lowered his head, eyes fixed on the intruder.

"He will attack if you take more time in putting the knife down."

The thief dropped his weapons.

"Kick them away." Sarah ordered.

The thief obeyed.

Smiling, she addressed her mechanical. "Buttons, stay here. If he decides to leave that spot, you may have him for dinner."

Alice walked into the kitchen and stopped when she saw what was happening.

Looking at the floor, Alice asked, "Shall I remove the weapons from the floor, Miss?"

"Please do."

The thief did not move; he kept his stare directly at Buttons, the mechanical never blinking.

Looking at the thief, Sarah added, "I'm going to fetch a constable, Alice. I should not be long."

The thief was shaking with a slight tremor and tears rolled down his cheeks.

"Yes, Miss. Shall I go and hang the laundry in the cellar?"

"Yes, Alice. Please continue with your normal duties."

"As for you, Mr. Intruder," Sarah said. "Now you will know the scare you tried to put me through."

Grinning, the maid went about her regular routine, walking an exaggerated circle around the thief as she went to the basement door.

"You can't leave me with that," the thief cried.

The only answer the thief heard was when Sarah said, "Ta ta," as the front door closed behind her.

Fur, *Feathers,* and Scales

He stared at Buttons and swore as the mechanical licked its lips.

Rama and the Camel

Will Wright

Rama's father's birthing day was in two days, and she had nothing to give him. She'd heard stories of genies that granted wishes when you rubbed an oil lamp. If she could find a genie, she could get her father a mountain of gold or a great palace. Rama loved her father very much and wanted to give him something he would like.

But she was too small to reach the lamp.

Being only six, she could only reach the candleholders, the water jar, the oil cruse, and the incense box. She considered each, but decided that, with her small hands, the incense box was best.

So, she took the incense box from the shelf and rubbed it.

She was glad there was no fire in the box, because as she rubbed, the box started getting warm. She was sure she had rubbed the box longer than the hero in the story had.

Shouldn't a genie have come out by now?

She kept rubbing the box.

She started rubbing after the morning meal and was still rubbing at noon. She stirred the soup with one hand while she rubbed the incense box with the other. At the table, she ate with one hand and kept the other beneath the table rubbing the little incense box. As she gathered the goats, she had to put down the goad to close the gate—she needed one hand to rub the incense box.

Lying in her blankets, she worried that she might fall asleep before the genie came.

Her left eye blinked, but she rubbed the incense box.

Her right eye drooped, but she rubbed the incense box.

Just when she couldn't stay awake another moment, the little box jumped in her hand, let off a puff of incense, and there on her blanket stood a man no bigger than Rama's little finger.

"I am the genie of the incense box," said the tiny man in a squeaky voice. "I grant you one wish."

Rama would have clapped her hands in glee, but her hands were too sore from rubbing the incense box all day. She set her face to her most adult expression and said, "I wish, for my dear father, a mountain of gold for his birthing day."

The genie crossed his arms, shut his eyes, and held his breath 'til he turned red . . . but nothing happened.

"I'm sorry mistress," he said. "I cannot bring a mountain of gold."

Rama was a little disappointed. She remembered hearing her father say, "Our lives will be wonderful when I find us a mountain of gold."

It was, perhaps, too much to wish from such a small genie. Still, there was one other thing her father desired.

She set her face to her most adult expression and said, "I wish, for my dear father, a great palace for his birthing day."

The genie crossed his arms, shut his eyes, and held his breath 'til he turned purple . . . but nothing happened.

"I'm sorry mistress," he said. "I cannot bring a great palace."

Rama and the Camel

Rama was even more disappointed. She remembered hearing her father say, "Our lives will be wonderful when we live in a great palace."

It was, perhaps, too much to wish from such a small genie.

Once again, she set her face to her most adult expression and asked, "What wishes can you grant for my dear father on his birthing day?"

The tiny genie bowed. "Great Mistress," he answered, "I can turn his nose into a clove of garlic."

Rama thought, but not hard. She didn't think her father would like his nose changed into a clove of garlic for his birthing day.

"I do not wish that," she told the genie.

The tiny genie bowed. "Great Mistress," he said, "I can turn his nose into a wad of wet wool."

Rama thought, but not hard. She didn't think her father would like his nose changed into a wad of wet wool for his birthing day.

"I do not wish that," she told the genie.

The tiny genie bowed. "Great Mistress," he said, "there is only one other magic I can do. I can make his camel smell any way you wish."

Rama thought, and this time, much harder than the other times. A camel can smell very bad indeed. Perhaps her father would like a sweet-smelling camel for his birthing day.

"I do wish that," she told the genie.

The little genie crossed his arms, shut his eyes, and held his breath 'til he turned blue.

"It is done, Mistress," he said, and disappeared in a little puff of incense.

Rama woke early the next morning. Though her father's birthing day was still a day away, she decided to surprise him with a good-smelling camel a day early.

Fur, *Feathers,* and Scales

"Jasmine," she said aloud. She crossed her arms, closed her eyes, and held her breath as she had seen the genie do. "I wish the camel to smell like jasmine."

She hurried to wash and dress herself. She couldn't wait to see how her father would like his surprise.

When she got to the table, she greeted her mother. Her father was outside tending the animals.

What if the genie lied to her or couldn't do what he promised? He was such a tiny genie. Perhaps even the wish of changing the camel's smell was too great for him.

Father entered the house. He looked angry.

"Papa!" called Rama.

"One moment, dear Rama," he answered. He turned to Mother. "Did you hear anyone moving around the animals last night?"

"No," Mother answered. "I would have wakened you."

"Someone," Papa said, "has played a trick on me. He has spilled perfume all over the camel. How can I do my business at the bazaar with a camel that smells like flowers?"

It had not occurred to Rama that her father would prefer a camel that smells like a camel. If only she could take back her wish.

What had the genie said?

"I can make his camel smell any way you wish."

Perhaps, if she wished it, the camel would go back to normal.

She crossed her arms, closed her eyes, and held her breath. Silently she thought, "I wish the camel to go back to normal."

Rama went about her chores without her normal enthusiasm. She was tired and disappointed. She had gotten a wish and wasted it. She should have known her father wouldn't want a camel that smelled of jasmine. She didn't even know if her second wish had changed the camel back.

Rama and the Camel

Her father returned from the bazaar at dusk. She walked out to the pen to smell the camel for herself. Her father was feeding the animals when she arrived.

"I can do that, Papa," she said.

Her father looked at her. "Maybe you are big enough. What a helpful little daughter I have." He patted her on the head. "Make sure you're inside before dark."

The feed sacks were heavy, but Rama managed to pour feed for the goats and draw water for the trough. She put fresh hay in the manger.

She went over to the camel and took a good sniff. All she smelled was camel.

"It was a silly thing to wish a camel to smell of jasmine," she said.

"I liked smelling that way."

Rama had never heard the camel speak before, nor any other animal. She had been pretty sure that animals couldn't talk like humans did. Still, the camel had just spoken to her.

She was only six; there were probably a lot of things she didn't know.

"You like jasmine?" she asked.

"It's a lot better than how I usually smell," the camel replied. "Though I think I like the smell of lemons better."

Rama crossed her arms, closed her eyes, and held her breath. "I wish for you to smell like lemons," she said.

Instantly the pen was filled with the delicious smell of lemons. It was very strong, but not overpowering.

"Ah yes," said the camel. "That's very nice."

Rama agreed, but she still liked jasmine better.

She was just about to wish the camel back to normal again, when a large group of people she'd never seen before came over the hill from the north. The crowd went right up to the animal pen where she and the camel were standing. They were holding shovels and pickaxes and rock drills, and every one of them had a clove of garlic for a nose.

"Since the day we were cursed," said the first person to reach the pen, "I have smelled nothing but garlic. Now, I can smell lemons."

"We all smell lemons," another agreed.

"I never thought I would smell something so wonderful again," added a third.

"Is it you, child, that I'm smelling?" asked the first.

"No," Rama replied. "It is this camel."

"We are gold miners," said the first. "If we dig gold for you all night, may we sit by this wonderful camel during the day?"

Rama knew she should ask her father, but here was a way of getting a real present for him. If she asked permission, it would ruin the surprise.

"I agree," she said.

The miners went to their work.

"If father comes and smells lemons," said Rama, "he may think someone has tricked him again."

"It is true," said the camel. "You should wish me back to normal."

"I will return in the morning," promised Rama, "and you will smell of lemons then."

Rama woke before the dawn and rushed out to the pen to see the camel. Next to the pen lay a mound that sparkled even in the deep blue predawn.

"Good morning, Rama," the camel greeted her politely.

"Good morning, Camel," she replied. "Are you ready to smell like lemons again?"

"There's no hurry. It's not day yet," said the camel. "I've been thinking. I also like the smell of cinnamon a lot. Can we try that?"

Rama and the Camel

"Oh, I like cinnamon, too," said Rama. She crossed her arms, closed her eyes, and held her breath. "I wish for you to smell like cinnamon," she said.

Instantly the pen was filled with the delicious smell of cinnamon. It was very strong, but not overpowering.

"Ah, yes," said the camel. "That's very nice. I like it as much as I like the smell of lemons."

Rama agreed, but she still liked jasmine better.

She was just about to wish the camel to smell of lemons, when a large group of people she'd never seen before came over the hill to the south. The crowd went right up to the animal pen where she and the camel were standing. They were holding hammers, and trowels, and chisels, and every one of them had a wad of wet wool for a nose.

"Since the day we were cursed," said the first person to reach the pen, "I have smelled nothing but wet wool. Now I can smell cinnamon."

"We all smell cinnamon," another agreed.

"I never thought I would smell something so wonderful again," added a third.

"Is it you, child, that I am smelling?" asked the first.

"No," Rama replied. "It is this camel."

"We are palace builders," said the first. "If we build a palace for you all day, may we sit by this wonderful camel at night?"

Rama knew she should ask her father, but here was a way of getting a second present for him. If she asked permission, it would ruin the surprise.

"I agree," she said.

Rama's father was surprised to find a large group of people sitting in his animal pen all day, and a different group at night, but as he saw the beginning of a great palace, and the beginning of a mountain of gold, he didn't seem to mind.

Rama found that her father was right. Things were wonderful living in a palace with a mountain of gold. Many things were different, but as she and her parents still loved each other, the best parts of her life remained the same.

The builders and miners were happy, her parents were happy, and even the camel was happy, with all his new friends, and smelling like lemons during the day, and cinnamon at night.

And during dusk and dawn, when it wasn't fully day, nor was it fully night, and the world was most beautiful, Princess Rama rode out among the hills on her wonderful camel that smelled of jasmine.

Recycled

Jerome W. McFadden

Jasper had no idea where he was or how he got there. It looked like a massive airplane hangar with separate lines of people standing in alphabetical order, if you judged by the large panels overhead that read A, B, C, etc. The panel above his head read D. No one in the lines spoke. Each row shuffled forward at a snail's pace to a bank of desks where attendants seemed to be briefing people before someone came to escort them away. Some of the folks argued and screamed when they were pulled away, while others followed their guides with beatific smiles on their faces.

Another handful of attendants was walking between the long lines, calling out names while glancing now and then at their clipboards. To add to the weirdness, all of the attendants behind the desks and on the floor were wearing togas like the ancient Romans, while the folks standing in the lines were in modern clothes, more or less. It had to be some kind of international terminal because people were dressed in blue jeans, tennis shoes, T-shirts, suits, dresses, and skirts, but also in burkas, djellabas, hijabs, berets, kippahs, caftans, African kangas, and on and on. Neither the attendants nor the people in the lines looked happy.

Jasper heard his name being called. A short, fat, balding guy in a wrinkled toga, looking overworked and underpaid, was scuffling along Jasper's line in sandals, repeating Jasper's name. Jasper held his hand up, waving at the man. The little guy stopped beside him, glancing at his clipboard, then back at Jasper. "J. Deol?"

"Jasper Deall," Jasper replied.

The man looked back at his clipboard. "You don't look like your photo."

"Let me see it," Jasper said, reaching for the board. The little guy snatched it away from him. "New arrivals are not allowed to look at their files. Everybody knows that."

"Well, excuse me, but I don't know that. Who the hell are you, and why do you have a file on me? And where am I? I don't remember coming here."

"Watch your language. And what do you remember?"

Jasper reflected for a moment. *What did he remember? Good question.* "I was driving on Interstate 80 West, on my way to Tannersville. Snow and ice. The eighteen-wheeler in front of me, one of those big 52-footers, jackknifed right in front of me, going sideways, and I was pumping my brakes like a mad man and going into a skid, and . . ."

"And how did that come out?"

Jasper thought for a long moment, then slowly said, "Oh . . . damn."

"Watch your language. And now that we have that settled, you are now at the Admittance & Selection Center, and I am your Admittance Counselor. So, come with me."

"Where are we going?"

"Reincarnation and Transmigration Control."

"Uh, reincarnation and . . .? Really? I never thought that was a real thing, you know?" Jason said.

The little fat man looked his clipboard again. "It says here that you are a Jainist."

"A Janice? Who's Janice? I don't know anybody named Janice."

Recycled

Baldy frowned. "Our files are rarely wrong, but we can verify later. Now, please, come along."

Jasper hesitated to step out of line. "Why aren't these folks coming with us?"

"They are not Jainists. They are Christians, Muslims, Jews, and that sort of thing. Their programs are different."

"But . . . I am . . . or was . . . an atheist," Jasper said.

"We do not punish stupidity. We judge on life-long actions, behavior, morality. That sort of thing. And, of course, additionally, as a Jainist, on your layered karma spread over your previous lifetimes."

"My previous life . . ."

But the man did not bother to listen. He led Jason to a cubicle at the far end of the hangar. "Sit," he said, pointing to a chair.

The cubicle walls were lined with photos of animals—snakes, insects—and plants. On one wall was plastered a complex chart. Reams of papers cluttered Baldy's desk, with more files littering the floor.

"You, uh, look like you're a little behind in your paperwork," Jasper said.

"Behind? Behind? There are more and more of you. Every day, every year. More and more of you. You never quit populating. And all of you say you want to go heaven, but none of you are ever in a rush to get there. But at least with you people, Jainists, we do not have to worry about that, do we?"

"We don't?" Jasper said in a slightly worried voice.

"But you worry me, Mr. Deol," Baldy said to Jasper. "You seem to be ignorant of your Jainist background and yet you have a wonderful record. You are about halfway through your eight-point-four million birth cycles and always on an up-cycle."

"I don't know what you are talking about, but if you tell me who this Janice is, maybe I'll remember her and that will explain it."

Baldy stood up, clutching Jasper's folder. "I am going to talk to my supervisor to see if I can sort this out. You wait here."

Jasper watched the man disappear, then stood up to inspect the chart on the wall. The title said *Gatis* in bold print, with a list of strange words below it, each followed by an English translation in parentheses: *Deva* (Demigods), *Manusya* (humans), *Narakki* (hell beings), and *Tiryanca* (animals, plants, & micro-organisms). There were four *Gatis*, each with four corresponding layers. Jasper was pleased to see that the *Manusya* (humans) were the middle brackets, which seemed to be good. The *Narakki* seemed to have seven levels of hell. With a little luck, that Janice bitch, whoever she was, was not about to pull him down there with her.

Baldy came back in a few minutes, sweating, his face puffed and red as if his supervisor had given him a hard time. "You are not Jasbir Deol," he shouted, slamming the file on his desk.

"You asked me if I was J. Deall. I am Jasper Deall. J. Deall."

"I meant Jasbir Deol."

"Not my fault, old buddy. That mistake is on you."

"Well, we can't send you back now that you've seen all of this," the man said, gesturing at the chart and pictures on the walls as he plopped into his chair.

"So?"

"According to our records, you, Jasper Deall, throughout your lifetime, have continually been guilty of deception, fraud, falsehood, and feigned self-importance. Is all of that true?"

Oh, shit, Jasper thought. *Got me.*

Recycled

"In such a situation, we can only grant you rebirth as an animal or vegetable. Your choice."

An animal or a vegetable? That's a choice? "Animal," Jasper said.

"Which one?"

"You're the man with the chart and categories. But it's your mistake, so you owe me. No pigs, donkeys, or poodles. Something noble, you know, like an elephant or something."

"A white elephant? Jainist's love white elephants."

"Enough with Janice. We're past her."

"Make a choice," Baldly said, waving at the mass of papers overflowing his office. "I need to move on."

"A lion? Or a stag? Or a stud horse? A stud horse sounds really good."

Baldy was running his finger down a list of animals, checking out the number of populations on the side. "It is becoming very difficult, you know? You humans keep killing the animals off. Shooting them, trapping them, taking away their habitat, poisoning the waters, eating them, on and on. And when they die, they flat out refuse to become humans. Can't blame them, I suppose. How about becoming an ant? We have lots of ants."

"Forget it. Let's do the stud horse thing. I like the thought of that."

"You don't deserve that. Best thing I can give you, given your record, is a male elephant."

"Elephants live a long time, don't they?"

Baldy sighed as if he had other things to do. "Yes, about as long as you humans, if they are not poached for their tusks."

"So, let's do an elephant."

"Wild or tame? In Thailand and Cambodia, the elephants are feed, washed, and treated well but they have to work. In East Africa, they run wild and free, but if you have a nice set of tusks, you'll probably be poached and then turn back up here very shortly. And neither you nor I want to go through this again so soon. We have elephants who run wild along the coasts of West Africa, but most of them are in the coastal deserts. A bit hot and thirsty, but nobody bothering you."

"Bull elephant. East Africa."

Baldy sighed. "Why am I not surprised."

"But I have a question. Will I remember all of this? My former life and this little misunderstanding?"

Baldy sat back in his chair. "So you can come back to pester me again? Negotiate a better life just because I made one mistake?"

Saw me coming, Jason thought. "No. Just asking," he lied.

Baldy stood up. "Follow me, please, to Transmigration Control, and we will send you on your way."

Jason stood up to follow him. But he could not resist adding, "Please say hello to Janice, who-ever-she-is. She sounds like she'd be fun. But, damn, I don't remember her."

"Watch your language."

The Dignity of Man

Jeff Baird

"Cody, stop jumping. You're going to wake the whole house!"

I stroked the soft head of my energetic, year-old, Siberian Husky puppy. "Let me finish my coffee, and then we'll go for a ride to your happy place." No sooner did I utter those words, than her furry tail wiggled wildly.

Her particular happy place was the Lehigh River Canal Park in Allentown, Pennsylvania, which runs between the Lehigh Valley Railroad and the Lehigh River. The park is on the site of what was once a part of the Lehigh Canal, built in the early nineteenth century to transport coal and other minerals from Carbon County to the ports of Philadelphia. Today, it is a beautiful walking and biking path, and I have spent many a day walking, running, and biking this historic trail.

For pet owners, it's a wonderful place because it is very secluded. Once we get to the trail, it opens up with a view of the glistening, rushing Lehigh River on one side. As you come up the hill, a grove of trees runs parallel to the gravel-covered path. As the railroad cars run past, it is not hard to imagine the days when the adjoining canal shipped cargo through the locks that raised and lowered the level of water. Acting as natural boundaries, the railroad tracks, the canal, and the river form a perfect area to walk your pets. If a dogwalker chose their time properly, they could have the trail pretty much to themselves. This was just fine for training Cody basic commands and to allow her to be off leash.

On this cool, sunny, late-fall day, the trees displayed their magical, many-hued foliage, and the air was crisp with a hint of the season to come. Cody enjoyed her freedom, checking out some nearby trees.

Up ahead of us, I spotted a bike rider slowly riding toward me as he came around a nearby blind curve. I knew Cody would be curious.

"Cody, come!" I called out her recall command.

Immediately, she sprinted to my right side and assumed the sit/stay position as she had been trained to do.

Pausing for a moment to let the command sink in, I reached down to the top of her head and playfully rubbed her pointy ears. This, in turn, caused her to look up at me with her beautiful, blue eyes.

"Good girl, good girl," I repeated a few times and handed her a treat that she took gently out of my hand, her tongue licking both sides of her snout.

"Good girl," I said again as I lovingly stroked her perked-up ears to reinforce the training.

Once the bike had passed, I rewarded her with another treat after I made sure the rider did not appear to be a threat or distraction.

Pausing again for effect on her hold position.

"Okay, Cody, good girl." I gave her the release command so that she could go traipsing off into the forest and sniff away to her heart's content.

However, for whatever reason, my little fluffball of a puppy decided that she was going to investigate the smell or the motion of the stranger. By now, this bicycle rider had passed us some twenty seconds or more ago. Cody started trotting toward him. At first, I didn't think that there was

The Dignity of Man

going to be a problem because, even though she was just a puppy, she was very good at obeying her commands.

I gave her the recall command. "Cody, come!" Unfortunately, she just kept on casually trotting along.

"Cody, come; Cody, come!" I repeated multiple times, each command at increasing volume.

For whatever reason, Cody had it in her head that she was going to follow this unfamiliar curiosity. She just kept trotting, not sprinting, so I casually started jogging after my stubborn little Husky. I still held the illusion of being able to mimic my former track-star self.

It didn't take me long to realize that there was no way I was going to catch up to either of them. It must have been pathetically comical if anybody had been there to see this. For someone who used to be as fast as the wind, for someone who used to have the nickname "RoadRunner," to be lagging so far behind reminded me how many years had passed. Surely now they would be calling me "Coyote," watching me vainly try to run after them.

"Stop. Hey, you riding the bike, *stop!*" I tried in vain to get his attention. "Come here, girl. Here, Cody, come! Hey, you, please stop. My puppy is chasing you. She won't hurt you. *Please stop!*"

With each phrase, my adrenaline increased. To my frustration and anger, he didn't stop. But he'd heard me at last. I know because he turned and gave me the finger.

To this day, I don't understand what made him do that. Maybe he was afraid of dogs. Maybe he thought I was yelling at him for some feigned trail rage and was far enough away that he felt safe in expressing his opinion. For whatever reason, he just kept riding away from me.

They were heading in the direction of the parking lot about a mile away. It took me about fifteen minutes to reach the parking lot. I could only hope that the rider would be at his car and that Cody would be there wagging her tail and patiently waiting for her master.

Unfortunately, she was nowhere to be found. As I stood there gasping for breath and turning my head every which way, frantically searching, I faced the unpleasant truth that the parking lot was deserted, and I was alone . . . without my puppy. While the Lehigh Canal is in the middle of a small city, it is situated in a pretty out-of-the-way area.

It was difficult not to think the worst. *Did she wander into the adjoining railroad yard? Did she continue on the road leading out of the park and reach some very busy and dangerous city streets?* Then the thought that was darkest in my mind: *Was she dognapped?* Cody was a pretty, one-year-old, pure Siberian Husky puppy. She would make for a fine prize for someone dealing in dogs. Tears quickly came to my eyes as I imagined all the terrible things that could befall my beautiful puppy.

As responsible dog owners, my family had tattooed all our dogs and embedded them with chipped ID tags. As we like to say, they partied one night and came home with a tattoo. In addition, she had a sturdy collar on, with her tags and ID. What she didn't have was what we today commonly refer to as GPS. This is a godsend to modern pet owners that was, unfortunately, unavailable to us at the time.

I got in my car and started driving around. Rolling down the car windows and searching.

"Ccccooooddddyyyy! Here, girl! Ccccooooddddyyyy!"

I was screaming at the top of my lungs for Cody to come back. Then stopping and being quiet and listening if I could hear other dogs that were barking as a signal that maybe she was nearby. I repeated this process of screaming and being silent over and over again. Sadly, all I heard was the occasional train chugging along the nearby railroad tracks. It had been over one hour since my little puppy wandered off when I went back down to the river and into the forest. I hoped she had found her way back.

As desperation washed over me, I decided to take a quick drive back home and see if by chance Cody had been able to find her way there. I pulled into the driveway and looked into the fenced in back yard, hoping against hope to see her familiar shape playing. She was not there. I walked into the house with a sense of dread, my mind a blank, not knowing what to do next. My family was still sleeping, and I didn't have a clue as to how I was going to explain that I had lost our beloved pet. I couldn't bear thinking about the look in my children's eyes once they heard the devasting news.

Fear overwhelmed me, and I almost didn't notice a dull ringing that got louder and louder with each passing moment. I lunged for the phone, praying it was a call about Cody. *Please don't hang up before I answer!*

"Hello," I gasped.

"Hello," replied a raspy voice.

In an uncertain tone with tears stinging my eyes, I said, "Can I help you?"

"Hey, did you lose a dog?" a high-pitched voice said.

Dumbstruck, I muttered, "What?"

"I got a dog here, and it has this phone number on its collar tag. Did you lose a dog?"

Finally, it dawned on me what the person—maybe a woman?—was saying, and I blurted out at the top of my lungs, "Oh, my god, *yes!*" A joyfulness washed over me at the realization that my little puppy dog had been found.

"Is she okay? Where is she? Is she safe?"

"Yeah, she's okay. You wanna come and get her?"

"Yes, absolutely, tell me where you are, and I'll come and get her right now."

The line seemed to go dead. "Hello, are you still there?" I said hesitantly.

Fur, *Feathers*, and Scales

"Ahh, yeah, she's fine, but it's a little out of the way; maybe I should meet you somewhere."

"No, no, it's okay; I'll come to you." Relief washed over me.

"Well, okay. Do you know where the railroad tracks cross over the Basin Street overpass near the river?"

"Yes, I'm not that far away," I said as I began to picture a map in my head.

"Okay, cross over the tracks and head toward the river. Look for the path that goes into the forest, and we'll meet you there."

"Can you give me a number to reach you in case I get lost? And here is my car phone number just in case."

"My phone is dead, I'm using someone else's phone, so I have to give the phone back."

"All right, I'm on my way. I should be there in twenty minutes or so. Thank you again so much." With a sense of urgency, I rushed out of my house and jumped into the car.

In my anguished state to get to Cody, it didn't dawn on me the vagueness of the directions. As I got closer to the location, I began to realize the strangeness of where I was headed. I thought of picking up my brand-new cellular phone in a bag to call home and tell them where I was going. If it had not been for the inconvenience of having to pick up a bag the size of woman's purse and pry loose the Velcroed cover while driving, I probably would have.

I came to a spot where I had to stop and get out of my car and blaze a trail into the unknown. All kinds of weird thoughts were running through my head as I tried to find a seemingly secret location. I could hear running water nearby and saw the railroad tracks disappear into the forest. As I was searching in this secluded area, I heard what sounded like a dog up ahead. The forest opened up, and the main road turned out to be just an overgrown deer trail. This ran along a branch of the river that had eroded, which made for a hidden location. Once I was onto this wooded embankment, there appeared to be old, abandoned, industrial dumpsters strewn across the clearing, randomly tossed about.

In this concealed makeshift shantytown were about a dozen homeless men and women milling about, petting Cody. The moment I saw Cody, I was elated. At the same time, I became aware of a very real sense of apprehension. To be honest, I was just plain scared at being in this very out-of-the-way location when no one knew where I was.

It didn't help settle my nerves when I noticed the way the residents were dressed. From what I could see, their clothes were tattered and disheveled with various forms of mismatched functionality. There was even one older, overweight man who had what looked to be women's clothing on—right down to bright blue pantyhose in lieu of pants, with women's panties on the outside.

When I approached the group of people huddled around Cody, I could see she had an improvised rope leash tied around her collar. The man holding the lead was dressed in a greasy, grimy, red snowsuit with an oversized, faded black watch cap. While it was late fall, the sun had warmed the air enough to be at odds with his cold weather gear. Beneath his scraggly, white beard, he had a pockmarked face with sunken, reddish cheeks. His teeth were rotted, which matched his overall appearance. It was, overall, a discomforting scene.

Once they spotted me, all eyes turned as we warily checked each other out. It didn't help that they looked like every movie cliché about the homeless you can imagine. After a few moments, the crowd parted, and Cody finally saw me. She pulled at the makeshift leash and barked, trying to get to me. Even though a puppy, her strong, Husky physique became quite evident as she pulled the guy in the snowsuit across the path to get to me.

Fur, *Feathers,* and Scales

I fell to my knees and embraced her as she licked my face and did head butts all over my body. Tears sprang from my eyes as I looked up at the homeless man with the tattered appearance. As I stood up, he handed the rope leash to me and introduced himself as Howard.

"She sure is a pretty doggy," he said in a high, squeaky voice that I had assumed was a woman during the earlier phone call.

"I can't thank you enough. You don't know what this means to my family."

"Don't worry about it. When she wandered into camp, I figured she belonged to someone. At first, she wouldn't come near me, but she finally warmed up to me and let me pet her. You're lucky. Her collar was ripped and ready to fall off. I had a hard time reading the phone number. It was real dirty."

As I stood there listening to him talk in that high-pitched voice, I began to realize how above and beyond this man had gone to reunite me with our beloved family pet. He told me how he had given Cody to a friend to watch while he went to find a pay phone to call me.

My mind went through some quick mental calculations about what he must have gone through. It was at least a mile to get to Center City, where I imagined the nearest phones would be located. Howard was such a gentleman, and he used money that I'm sure he didn't have in the first place to call to tell me that he had found our dear Cody.

By now, the dozen or so homeless people in the camp were surrounding me and petting Cody. All of them were talking to me at once, telling me how Cody had wandered into their camp.

"What a pretty doggie," said one woman with polka dot pajamas on under a bright pink, oversized vest.

"I used to have one just like her," said a man who had on at least three pairs of jeans.

The Dignity of Man

"What's her name? What's that you said? Connie? That's a strange name for a dog."

"No, it's Cody," I had to repeat.

"Don't worry, she can't really hear you unless you scream in her ear," said the woman in polka-dot pajamas.

After a few minutes in their company, I felt truly ashamed of my previous apprehension. These people were so nice. It was a very moving experience. I felt terrible when I realized, however, I had been out for a walk and only had a couple of dollars in my pocket to repay them for their kindness.

To shame me further, they refused to take what little money I had with me to offer them for their good deed.

Howard was standing off to the side of the group as I prepared to take Cody home. I walked over to him and reached into my pocket.

"No," he said as I pulled out a few one-dollar bills. "No, don't need it. Ain't no reason to give me money."

I looked at him and knew that it wasn't true, but I didn't know what else to do.

I gave them all one last look and said goodbye.

"Cody, sit. Cody, heel. Good girl! Okay, walk."

I felt all eyes on us, and I was so proud that now Cody was obeying her commands. Of course, if she had done this in the first place, I wouldn't have had the chance to meet them or have this heartwarming experience.

After I got Cody to the car, I hugged and kissed her over and over and repeatedly thanked God. While walking back through the forest to where my car was parked, I made the decision that it wasn't right to just walk away. I didn't care; I wasn't going to listen to them.

I made my way to an ATM and took out one hundred dollars. I then stopped at Dunkin Donuts on the way back and bought several dozen doughnuts. After which I returned to this homeless shelter carrying a big bag of doughnuts with Cody by my side. It was almost like she was prancing and eager to get back to her new-found friends.

I guess that they were surprised that I had returned. They were probably under the assumption that once I got out of there with what I needed, they would never see me again. It made me feel good inside to know that I had returned and that I was able to properly thank them for their good deed. I knew that the reward I gave them was minuscule compared with what they had done for me.

I sensed that Cody understood the significance of the moment and was strutting her stuff right next to me as I walked up to Howard. For his protection, I gave him a specific box of doughnuts that had the money hidden in the bottom of the box. I was fearful that if others saw him with the money, I would be putting him in danger.

I think he figured out that I was not going to say no, and that it was the right thing to do. However, as I turned my head around to get a last look, I was shamed once more as I watched him open the box of doughnuts and share the money with his companions. The expressions on all their faces melted my heart.

It has been many years now since this moving experience, and I have had many dogs since Cody passed over the Rainbow Bridge. All of us have gone to the Canal Park countless times, and each time I come home, I make sure to pass by the entrance to what I have now informally named Howard's home. I slow down and roll the window down, stroke my dog's head, and make a silent prayer of thanks.

Sadly, I read a few years ago that the city had closed this so-called park in order to redevelop the land for some new Starbucks or CVS. It reminded me of the selflessness and humanity these forgotten people had shown my family and our dog. It is a memory that has stayed with me all these years, and a tale that I hope stimulates many acts of kindness. For all of you, and especially Howard, thank you from

The Dignity of Man

the bottom of my heart and paws. You showed me the true dignity that we can all aspire to reach.

Missing the Point

Emily P. W. Murphy

"What time do they leave, again?"
"High noon."
"Oh, good. We have lots of time."
"Not as much as you think."
"We have all the time in the world."
"Stop gazing at your reflection. You're not even packed."
"What do I have to bring? We're going to be on a boat the whole time."
"Well, be sure to bring your horn."
"You really think you're funny, don't you?"
"Well, not to blow my own horn but . . ."
"Ugh. Enough with the horn puns. How long will we be gone again?"
"Over a month."
"That's a long time. Are you sure you want to go?"
"We're going, one way or the other. Besides, this place is no fun during the rainy season."
"It is a great time to get away, I'll give you that."
"And at least Becky will be there. You like her. She's a party animal."
"But she'll bring Jake, and he's such a weasel."
"Don't be a snob. Come on. Let's hurry. I want to get there early."

Fur, *Feathers,* and Scales

"Why? We'll just end up standing in line with all the other couples."

"I want to get a good spot on board."

"I guess you're right. I don't want to end up crammed in next to some old cow."

"Listen, we're taking this trip. We might as well enjoy it."

"That doesn't mean we have to board any sooner than necessary. We're going to be at sea forever. I just want to get something to eat before we go."

"We just had breakfast. You can't possibly be hungry. Grazing all day isn't good for you, you know."

"Don't body-shame me. Hey, are the Marlins coming?"

"Of course not. You know how they feel about boats."

"Right. Of course."

"But they might swing by later on."

"That would be nice."

"Do you know if Sarah is coming?"

"That bitch? I don't think so."

"What about Adam?"

"He's such a stud!"

"I hope he's not coming. I don't need to watch you staring at him for the rest of the month."

"Well, you said we should enjoy the trip."

"Besides, it's couples only, remember?"

"Right."

"Look at the time. We have to leave now."

"Okay, okay. Let's go."

"About time. It's starting to rain."

"Oh wait—I forgot my hat."

"Good."

"It's pouring out. I have to go back for it."

"They'll leave without us. Besides, you look ridiculous in hats. You don't have the head for it, and you know it."

"People always say I look great in that hat."

Missing the Point

"They say it, but then they laugh at you behind your back."

"Now you're just being mean."

"Okay, you've got your hat; now, let's run."

"I don't want to show up all sweaty."

"In this downpour, who will be able to tell? Come on, they'll leave without us."

"No, they won't."

"The instructions were very specific."

"Instructions are for *other* passengers. They *won't* leave without *us*."

"Why would you even think that?"

"Isn't it obvious? Even the organizer knows we're special. Unique. I mean, we're the guests of honor—the unicorns—you don't leave without the unicorns."

"They'd better not."

"They won't. Besides, even if they did, it's not the end of the world."

"Well, it would be for us. This is a once-in-a-lifetime opportunity."

"Fine, fine. I'm coming."

"Well, giddy-up then."

"I'm coming as fast as I can."

"*Well, go faster.*"

"Wait, my hat flew off."

"*Leave it!*"

"Bye, hat. . . . I really liked that hat."

"We're almost there. Mind those big puddles."

"I can hear the other passengers. But what's that other sound?"

"Uh—they're pulling up the gangplank. I told you we were going to be too late."

"But they can't leave without—"

"They're leaving."

"They must think we're already on board. What was the guy's name again?"

"Nathaniel? Nehemiah? No—no—Noah! That was it."

"Noah! We're not on board. Let us in. You forgot the unicorns."

"*I told you—*"

"Noooaaaahhh! I'm getting soaked!"

"*He can't hear you.*"

"He *has* to hear us."

"*He's inside that ship. It's solid Gopherwood. Besides, all those animals on board are making too much noise.*"

"Noooaaaahhh. Noooaaaahhh. Noooaaaahhh."

"*Are you done?*"

"It's starting to float away."

"*Well, they couldn't open the door now even if they wanted to. . . . Wait. Where are you going?*"

"I believe I'll go find my hat."

Inside the Tank

Jodi Bogert

Heron View Park's opening day was packed with people as usual, despite the overcast June skies. Chris was exhausted. His assignment that season was operating Blackbeard's Demise, the pirate adventure ride and Heron View's oldest attraction. All of Evergreen, Michigan, grew up on this ride and would pass on the experience to future generations. He never saw so many different kinds of people file in and out of the cars. Kids cried, couples argued, teens made out, and older people fell asleep.

Visitors traveled on winding tracks through dark tunnels where animatronic pirates stormed tropical beaches in search of buried treasure. At the end, a tank the size of a U-Haul truck revealed a sunken ship and a hoard of skeleton statues hidden in a dense, artificial sea kelp forest, sealing the pirate crew's dark fate. A salty smell of sea air and fish wafted from vents, making the experience lifelike. It was an honor for Chris to keep this ride going for another year. At one point during the day, he saw Heron View's owner, Mr. Cooperson, pass by with his clipboard and a smile, lifting his spirits.

Willie, the ride's previous operator and a descendant of Heron View's first owner, died just before season began.

Fur, *Feathers,* and Scales

It was not easy for employees to go about their usual business, especially for Chris. Willie was his neighbor and close friend. Chris's father died when he was a little boy, and Willie took it upon himself to help the small family, whether it was cooking the occasional meal or helping with yardwork. Over time, he became a regular during the holidays, and Chris considered him a second father. He believed that Willie had advice for everything, an answer for every problem: girls, school, and his life at home. When he started working at Heron View a few years ago, they ate almost every lunch break together; ham for Chris, tuna for Willie. Willie even taught Chris how to drive and helped him shovel driveways during the brutal winter months. Then last autumn, cancer showed up in Willie's lungs and spread rapidly, cutting his time shorter than anyone would have liked.

After learning about his diagnosis, Willie convinced Mr. Cooperson to hand the ride down to Chris. Mr. Cooperson revered him and placed the keys into Chris's hands shortly after the funeral. Both men that day nodded in understanding, no words needed.

At dusk, Heron View's employees shut down their attractions for the night. Chris stood at the podium and turned the silver keys to the left, parking the cars on the track. Chris passed through the exit gate and made his way around to the back of the ride, gazing at the outside mural of Blackbeard and his crew sailing across a raging sea. He and Willie painted it over the summer before sixth grade. Willie had arrived at Chris's front door one morning. Paint cans and brushes filled the back of his large, red pickup. "I decided that a blank wall isn't a good enough look," he said. "Would you like to paint a mural with me?" Chris looked at him and saw a flicker of a smile hidden behind his beard. The new artwork featuring the dastardly Blackbeard

Inside the Tank

attracted dozens of new riders that year. "And I have you to thank for it," Willie once told him.

Chris came to a small door and unlocked it using a small, gold key he wore on a chain around his neck. After locking himself in, he made his way up a steep staircase. At the top was a small walkway that led to the circular tank room. A deep rotting smell hit him hard in the face. He switched on the overhead lights and surveyed the disorganized chaos. An explosion of papers scattered all over a small desk. Maps of the Great Lakes and nearby Lake Heron spread over the walls, covered in red pins, planning a trail. Open books about all types of fish, both fresh and saltwater breeds, gathered dust. He opened one of the large coolers lining the edge of the tank. Cutlets of all types of fish overflowed the top. Thousands of dead fish eyes stared up at him. The small clock on the wall read 10 p.m.; it was Sybil's feeding time. If anyone told him the summer after high school he would be taking care of a mermaid, he would never have believed it.

He jumped when he heard a splash; light reflected from the water's surface and danced over the walls. He turned around and saw large, webbed hands with dark, hooked claws rise up from the water. She was hungry, as always. Chris knew he should be feeding her more, but he couldn't risk anyone noticing. Willie made him promise repeatedly that no one ever found out about her.

Chris put on heavy, rubber gloves and gathered a huge handful of fish. He tossed the pile into the water and waited. She shot out of the depths and thrashed around like a shark from a nature documentary hunting prey. Within seconds, the food was gone, and he tossed in serving after serving, watching her viciously devour. A splash of her large, dark tail signified her satisfaction, and he breathed a sigh of relief. He was not a fan of the sneaking around and looking after the beast, but he had no choice.

Fur, *Feathers,* and Scales

Later, while driving home in Willie's pickup, he thought about the night he first met her, when Willie ordered to meet him at the tank room. It was just after he learned about Willie's diagnosis, so his request to meet that night worried Chris. When Chris arrived, Willie handed him scuba gear and flippers. He pointed to the tank and told him to dive in. Chris wanted to ask a million questions. Yet, his curiosity got the best of him, and he obliged.

Sybil wasn't like the beautiful creatures he saw in Disney movies. When he saw her, he almost fainted from the shock. Her skin was stark white, caving in at her cheeks. Her arms were long and spindly, her rib cage stuck outward at her sides. Her strong, dark gray tail whipped around in the water. Gills fanned in and out as she breathed. Sharp teeth lined the inside of her mouth. Dark, stringy hair framed her pale face. She had no nose, and her eyes were black, void of emotion or warmth. She flexed her sharp, black claws and he gulped, paralyzed in disbelief.

A small light glowed on her forehead; a small hot spark of heat burned into Chris's forehead. Her thin lips stretched into a teeth-glinting smile as he jolted from the pain. *"My name is Sybil. Willie told me all about you. He told me that he would introduce you to me; he called it 'letting you in on the secret!'"* Her lips did not move, but Chris could hear her all the same, although he wished he didn't. Her high-pitched wail of a voice was not comforting to hear. Chris closed his eyes and told himself he was having a horrible dream. But as he opened his eyes, she was still there.

She frowned and looked downward; her eyes began to sadden. *"He's dying and will leave this earth soon. I know everything. He's entrusting you to look after me, even though I should tell you, I can take care of myself!"* She shoved her claws up to his face and gnashed her teeth. Flipping her tail, she swam away, and he went after her.

Inside the Tank

He found her, clinging to one of the skeleton statues. Scars trailed down her back, looking angry as the hands that inflicted them. She turned to him, and her face relaxed, though grief still reflected. Rubbing her eyes, she approached, studying him. Sybil pointed northward, in the direction of Lake Heron. *"I come from there..."*

She encircled the skeleton statue, looking at it with loathing. *"My husband was a leader of my people, but he was filled with foolish pride. People were dying from poisoned water. We had to travel upriver, find another home. But he would never admit to reason or that he was wrong, so my people suffered, including my younger sister."*

She waved a hand and conjured a shadowy figure of a lifeless mermaid. The small, limp body fell in between them, disappearing as it hit the ground. Everyone in town knew about the lake; the water grew more polluted each year. No one had been able to swim or fish in it for years. *"I confronted him, but he was filled with too much rage from how his people lost all faith in him. He attacked me."* She took the skeleton's head in her grasp, ripped it off as if it were wet clay, and threw it down on the ground, shattering it. *"I killed him. No one kills my sister, my people, and attacks me, his wife, and gets away with it."*

Sybil's black eyes flashed red with anger. Chris shuddered. She killed her husband, who was probably stronger than she, from sheer will. What was Willie thinking? Chris did not regard him as reckless. They looked up to the surface and saw Willie's silhouette looking down.

Sybil smiled as she watched him. *"I was hiding in the reeds, feeling stranded after I escaped, being a fugitive in the eyes of my people. Willie found me when he walked up by the shoreline. I told him what happened, and he said he could give me a place where I could disappear."*

She showed Chris a part of the tank's wall, filled with tally marks. In total, she had been here for almost a year.

Fur, *Feathers*, and Scales

Not even Mr. Cooperson was the wiser. He thought about how Willie's mind probably went through an unbelievable amount of stress daily, hiding her away from prying eyes, which was the last thing he or any sane person needed.

Chris got out of the tank, took off his scuba gear, and grabbed a towel sitting on top of a cooler. Drying off, he had no idea what he was going to do or if he was hallucinating. He made a vow never to go near her again. He didn't like her sharp teeth or the dull reflection in those dead eyes. Willie sat by the desk, his head in his hands. "Of all days I chose to try and pick up litter at that eyesore of a lake! I need you Chris. I don't think I will be around for much longer. I need you to look after her," he said. "She can never return now, after what happened. But I think that this could be the answer." He spread out a map of Lake Michigan, around a day's drive from town. It was big enough where she could disappear and start her life anew. "I'm sorry, Chris, but I need you to promise me that you will help her. Please?"

Chris wanted to protest, but he looked into the face of the pleading, old man. He agreed, and they shook on it. Throughout the following months, they met at night, completing numerous tasks, including waterproofing the back of the pickup with rubber and registering it in Chris's name. "I don't think a baby pool is going to work this time around," Willie said to him. Chris raised his eyebrows at him, and they both laughed for what felt like the first time in a long time. Willie also taught him how to act like everything was normal, a small but crucial part of the plan.

As Willie's condition grew worse, Chris spent a lot of his time at his hospital bedside. The last time they spoke, Willie held Chris's hand and smiled. "Thank you," he whispered. "Everything will be fine." Chris nodded, assuring his dear friend that he would see things through. However, he never had the heart to tell Willie that he wasn't doing it for her. Something about her was unnerving, beyond her looks, but he couldn't figure out what it was.

When Chris's mother announced in August that she would be staying at his grandmother's home in Grand Rapids over the upcoming weekend to help organize her attic, his stomach twisted. Now was the chance, and he had to take it. He waved goodbye to her as she drove away Friday evening, and the minute her car was gone, he threw up from nerves. He swallowed his overwhelming fear and drove to Heron View with enough food for himself, a small cooler of fish for Sybil, maps, and the garden hose in tow, praying that everything would turn out fine. When he arrived, he parked by a water pump located by the janitor's shed. He hooked up the hose and turned the knob. Water slowly filled the back of the pickup and he sprinted to the ride. He unlocked the rear door, ran up the stairs, and went over to the edge of the tank.

"Sybil? Can you hear me? It's time to go. Trust me, everything will be fine!" he called out. The water was still, very unlike her. She was usually restless when he came to feed her, splashing and flooding water everywhere. He leaned forward and looked down, trying to see what was keeping her. He just wanted to get the journey over with and go back to being like everyone else, tired of keeping this locked up inside him. "I never wanted this, you know. I never liked you," he called out, finally admitting it aloud.

Chris felt the hot flash of pain in his forehead, and his ears rang. *"Neither did I!"* Sybil screeched. Her hands lunged up to the surface and grabbed his ankles. He fell in headfirst, sinking into the depths. He felt around for something to grab onto. Bubbles and dark shadows clouded his vision, and his head roared with a blinding ache. Panic filled his body, wondering what was going on. Before he could think to scream, everything went black.

The water of the tank turned red. Sybil feasted on Chris's remains, filled with triumph and pride at her ability to fool not only one but two humans.

She would have never made it as a lone wolf, an outcast from the colony in the dark, rancid lake. She had to think of a plan for survival, a way for things to work out in her favor with little effort. Growing up, she had heard stories about human men who fell for females of her kind, and her idea grew from there. There were so many roles to choose from, a singing siren or a mysterious water maiden. She chose the unconventional role of a martyr, filled with scars, sympathy, and wisdom, complete with a thrilling, but false, backstory. Her reward would be easy prey.

She knew Chris had a family; he mentioned his pathetic mother and dead father to her in the past. Someone would come along to find him. All she had to do was sit and wait for the chance to strike again. More food would come along; no more surviving on scraps. Looking down at her claws, filled with fresh meat, she smiled. Fishing for humans was all too easy.

Man's Best Friend

DT Krippene

Zoran adjusted the orbital station's holographic wall display to admire puffed clouds drifting inside the azure atmosphere of Earth. Over fifty-thousand years ago, it was once home to millions of diverse species. Initial research crews on the surface discovered some survived the cataclysm after humanity fouled its own nest and turned the planet into a toxic dust bowl. In that very distant past, Zoran's ancestor escaped with a few thousand lucky inhabitants and their genetically enhanced pets to Salvuserit, a habitable exoplanet near Proxima-B.

"Look at you now. Time heals all wounds," he wondered in awe, quoting a line from an ancient text.

The entrance door warbled. "Enter," he said.

A uniformed courier from the surface exploration team ambled in, eyes glued to a tablet in her hand. "Dr. Zoranther Jinmaleekwa? Quarantine Ring requested your authorization for a special shipment."

She had to be new. Most people avoided his tongue-twisting name and called him Dr. Jin. Zoran took the tablet and scanned it. "Why are they bringing a live specimen here?"

Fur, *Feathers*, and Scales

The courier shrugged and slicked white hair strands against a head of mostly brown hair. "I don't know, sir. I just run errands."

Zoran sighed with a headshake. The tablet beeped when the biometric scan concluded.

"Just what I need," he muttered after the courier left.

He had planned to leave early for a big date tonight. The mere thought of Meeroon Sagetazi quickened his breath. A visiting senior journalist from the Media Network Consortium, she had the most recognized face in the business. It started as an interview about his work and ended with her wanting to know him better.

I'll stop at receiving on the way, then I'm gone. He switched off the live feed of Earth and slid a coverall suit over his clothes.

It normally took less than ten minutes to get there on the station's transivator. Heavy user traffic on the ten-story orbital ring the size of a small metropolis lengthened the ride to Receiving Deck by an extra fifteen minutes. The portal slid open, and the instant cacophony of harried container handlers crisscrossing the cavernous warehouse made Zoran fumble for communication earbuds.

"Over here," a voice spoke inside his ears.

Zoran weaved and ducked toward a smudged brown uniform worn by a dark-haired, squat fellow with a flattened nose that suggested he faceplanted walls for sport.

"Dr. Jin," the deck chief said in the rasped voice of someone who spent too much time yelling.

"I don't have much time, Boonto. Where is it?" He flinched when Boonto yelled toward a square-jawed loader with broad shoulders and muscular chest straining the snaps of his uniform.

The loader wheeled a sealed trunk, dropped a loading tablet atop the container, and pumped Zoran's hand. "Such an honor. Never thought I'd meet the Earth Reclamation

Director himself," he gushed in a dopey voice reminiscent of a character in a children's entertainment center.

Boonto grabbed the loader's arm. "Hey, easy on the doc. You'll break his poxin hand."

Zoran rubbed his fingers to bring life back to them and activated the trunk's control module. A meter-long, dirt-encrusted, orange-haired creature stared back at him in the holographic display above the container.

Sensing Zoran's presence, it spoke in a yowling, squeaky voice. "Eyowdo. Dowdee owtay. Friyow. Heembryato."

"Wonderful. Those things are talkers?" the loader carped.

"I've seen one of these before," Boonto chuckled. "Think they call it a koot or something."

"I believe the term is *cat*," Zoran corrected, bristling at the sight of it. Of all the creatures to survive, why did members of the Felidae family make the cut?

One of many bad ideas fomented by Earth's previous inhabitants, pets of all types were genetically modified for human speech to offer a means for owners to communicate with their charges. The enhancements didn't stop there, and no one considered long-term effects of forced evolutionary augmentation. This one had opposable thumbs and had to be four times larger than its forbearers portrayed in the archives. Zoran didn't need to check the volatile organics analysis to know it stank as well.

"Team that sent it wants to know what language it's speaking," Boonto said. "They got standing orders to identify lingual skills upon discovery—figured you know a couple dozen ancient tongues from the time, and you're kind of an expert."

"Just because I happen to temporarily foster a *talker*, doesn't mean I'm an expert on every mutant beast that still lives down there."

Fur, *Feathers*, and Scales

A sore subject, ever since a former girlfriend begged him to babysit a rescue talker she'd found, then cut off the relationship a week later. Zoran was now stuck with it. He made a mental note to call station services to kennel it before Meeroon Sagetazi showed up.

"They have AI translators for this. Why are you coming to me?" Zoran groused. He tapped on the trunk. "Hey there, fuzz ball, are you talking feral stuff we haven't transcribed yet?"

"Dowboo mierda," it meowed.

"Ah. Sounds like a variant dialect rooted to an old Earth Latin language called Spanish. Said it was cold and wondering where it is." Zoran didn't mention it needed to poop.

"Whatever you do, don't open it until it gets to Quarantine Ring." He switched off the holograph. "It needs to be released in a quarantine pod with cellulosic shred before it defecates in the container. I seem to recall reading that this species is rather finicky about messing its living space." *Unlike Earth's former inhabitants.*

Boonto saluted and beckoned the loader to follow with the trunk. Zoran sighed. Could have been worse, like the specimen they brought in from a congregation of alligator talkers they discovered in an underground river system. *Who in the dark-mattered pox thought I'd understand vocabulary based on bellows and hisses?* He considered himself lucky and headed for a little-used maintenance transivator in hopes of avoiding further interruptions.

He had to ready himself for the most ravishing female within four light years.

The moment the suite door opened, Zoran reeled from an odor of unprocessed diarrhea.

"Heerbo," he shouted.

Man's Best Friend

Out waddled a thinly furred, ape-like creature on two-legs, waving its arms in glee. "Zoree, Zoree," it shrieked.

They ended up on the floor in a knot of tangled limbs when Heerbo tackled him. Zoran extricated himself from Heerbo's overzealous embrace. Two neighbors had stopped in the hallway and scowled at Heerbo's joyful hooting guffaws through the open door.

Zoran punched the access panel to close it. "How many times have I asked you not to jump on me?"

Heerbo flashed stained teeth to smile. "Happy—you home."

"How did you get out of your room?"

"Learn push dot." Heerbo loped on all fours and jiggled the coded door latch with pride. "Watch you."

Damn thing is getting smarter every day. The day he found a permanent habitat for Heerbo couldn't happen fast enough.

Zoran eased the room door open and tripped on an untouched metal food bowl. He tried not to inhale. "Did you poop in the corner again?"

Heerbo's mouth drooped. "Use special chair like teach."

Entering the toilet room, Zoran's eyes watered. "Why isn't it auto flushing?"

A jet-like suctioning whoosh swallowed the offending waste, followed by a spritz of sterilizer and floral scent—which made it smell as if Heerbo pooped in a garden.

Suspicion trickled to his thoughts when he spotted dark streaks on the floor. "Did you *sit* on special chair while you pooped?"

Heerbo crouched and lowered its head. "Don't like feel of big wind. Sound scary. Moved poop to chair—after."

Zoran sniffed Heerbo's hand and winced. "Forever livin' pox, into the shower, now."

Heerbo lit up with a smile and galloped toward the adjoining bay. "Like shower, like shower."

Robed, hair still dripping from monkey-shower wrestle-mania, Zoran ambled wearily toward the kitchen with Heerbo behind him.

The refrigerator door was open. Broken packaged food containers littered the floor. He groaned at the sight of the appetizer plate he'd paid too many credits for, empty of exotic victuals for Meeroon.

"You ate all of . . ." Zoran sputtered. "You know you're not supposed to eat my food."

"Hungry," Heerbo whined.

"I left food in your room."

"Zordee food smell better."

"You'll get sick."

"I not sick."

Zoran extracted his palm-tablet and punched it with angered frustration.

"Good evening, Dr. Jin," a voice at station services answered. "I'm Phyla Brasiloo, shift manager. How can I assist you?"

"Someone was supposed fetch my . . ." Zoran glowered at Heerbo cowering in the kitchen corner. "Foster charge for kenneling."

"Oh," Phyla replied. "Uh, the reason might be the problem in quarantine. A large carnivore got out of its cage somehow. One of those talkers got the other talker animals riled up about being forced to eat vegetarian food. All handlers were ordered to Quarantine Ring."

Oh, no, not again. "Phyla, I'm expecting an important visitor and really need for someone to come take it."

"I'll look into it, sir, but it may take a while."

He glanced at the time display. Meeroon was due in less than two hours, of which he'd need every second to clean.

Man's Best Friend

"Thank you, Phyla. Just do your best. And please send a housekeeping bot, posthaste?"

Zoran clipped a few stray hairs on his ears after polishing his teeth, fighting fatigue from tidying up the suite himself. The housekeeping bot had become Heerbo's new friend to molest, which rendered it useless to the task. Thankful for small favors, he was relieved when Heerbo decided to take a nap afterward. Zoran made sure to change the lock code and immobilize the door open a crack in case Heerbo had another episode.

He buttoned a favorite shirt he saved for special occasions, chose a brushed microfiber, asteroid-silver suit coat, and examined himself in the mirror. Was it overkill? What if the evening turned out to be nothing more than a follow-up interview?

He selected a few excellent wine vintages on the bar, along with a couple of high-end liquors from home in case Meeroon was into the hard stuff.

The security module warbled. Someone from animal services he hoped; he yanked open the door with a few choice words about their tardiness.

The tall, shapely slenderness of Meeroon Sagetazi stood in his entryway. Hip-length, flowing white hair shimmered a rainbow of sparkles. Her irises were as blue as Earth's tropical oceans. Precious gem studs glinted on her delicate ears. It stole the breath from him.

"Oh—ah—hello," Zoran stuttered.

Meeroon tilted her head with a pixyish smile. "Is this a bad time?"

"Please, you're most welcome," he beckoned.

As she passed, the scent of her nearly made him swoon. Zoran had to blink a few times to break the spell of troubled thoughts suspended in the intoxicating mist of her perfume.

The moment ended with a body-slamming thunk against Heerbo's door, followed by piteous whining.

"Goodness," Meeroon tittered in the most delightful manner. "I thought you lived alone."

"Um, it's a foster pet. Belongs to someone on the surface. Please, be seated." He beckoned to a plush, silver satin couch and cringed when another thump resonated from Heerbo's room. He took a deep breath to keep from going into panic mode. "May I offer you a beverage?"

Meeroon removed her pollen-yellow jacket and offered it to him. Another wave of her sumptuous perfume made his eyes cross with desire. Frozen by her beauty, he stared at the shape-clinging powder blue slacks on her impossibly slim waist and golden silk blouse covering a broad chest.

"Sparkling water, please," she breathed with a sultry smile.

Zoran went to the bar to prepare drinks and swallowed an extra-large shot of Mapelsandra Bark liquor to steady his apprehension. He poured a glass of purified Mars water and added a cube of pressurized ice from an uncontaminated glacier, extracted miles beneath the Earth's surface. The ice popped and fizzled as he handed it to her. He sat on the opposite end of the couch, clutching his amply refilled tumbler.

"To the reclamation of Earth," he toasted.

Meeroon seductively sipped her drink, peering at him over the rim of her glass.

A beseeching howl arose through the open sliver of Heerbo's room.

"Sounds awfully sad," Meeroon said. "I didn't read you as an animal lover."

"It's a rather recent development." He took a generous swig. "Temporary situation, actually. I'm still trying to find it different lodgings."

"Zoreeeeeeeeeee . . ." Heerbo wailed.

"You have a talker?" Her face lit up with mirth. "*Oh, Zoree,*" she teased.

A muffled burp replaced Heerbo's doleful moans, followed by a gurgled back-flush and wet splatter.

Zoran exhaled a long, tortuous sigh.

Meeroon took another sip. "Goodness. Your foster may need looking after."

"I'll be right back." He tossed his drink down and pulled on the hem of his suit coat as if to do battle.

He actuated the door open a bit further to ensure the hairy troublemaker didn't bolt out the door. Heerbo cowered in the opposite corner, softly crying. Zoran tapped the lock code to seal the door and stepped around a puddle of stomach effluent, willing himself not to add to its volume.

Hands on hips, he towered over Heerbo's fetal-positioned curl. "This is what happens when you stray from your special diet."

"I sorry," Heerbo whimpered.

Zoran turned his eyes to the ceiling and found no answers. The evening was a certain disaster; no sense in making things worse. He helped Heerbo stand. "Come on, let's get you cleaned up—again."

Heerbo shuffled on all fours toward the shower with an arched back of anguish. Two-rinse cycles with essence of Willow Birch, Zoran left Heerbo in the cyclo-dryer set on gentle while he mopped up the mess. He took his time to give Meeroon the opportunity to make a dignified exit if she so chose.

"Let's put your pants on," Zoran said.

"Scratchy," Heerbo whined.

Fur, *Feathers*, and Scales

"I can't have you galivanting about with exposed–nether regions."

"Why care? Send Heerbo away."

"I'll find a nice home for you. I promise." Zoran stretched the pants as encouragement.

"Like home with you." Heerbo sniffled. "Love—you."

Zoran swallowed hard. How could a simple beast, talker or not, hold such affection in so little time. He hadn't done anything to deserve it other than board it, provide nutrition, adequate medical care, brush hair, talk to it—a calming massage on the neck whenever Heerbo was scared. *I'm too busy—can't get attached to this.* Heerbo needed a place with someone who'd offer it more attention.

Meeroon's voice called through the intercom. "Dr. Jin? Everything all right in there?"

Heerbo dashed for the door and punched buttons on the access pad with the nimbleness of a concert piano artist.

Little bastard saw me change the code. "Heerbo. No!"

Too late, Heerbo tackled Meeroon when the door slid open. Zoran grabbed Heerbo by the waist and yanked him off. Meeroon sputtered and coughed, splayed on her back with goggled eyes.

"I'm so sorry," Zoran gasped. He pushed Heerbo to the side and pointed an angry finger to signify stay. "Kennel services were supposed to pick it up earlier."

Meeroon's ample chest heaved with rapid breathing. Zoran feared for her and the certainty of a scandal—molested by a mutant creature from Earth, broadcast to her expansive media network followers.

She coughed in repeated succession. Coughing changed to huffing, then to chortles, until she bellowed in laughter, clutching her abdomen. Zoran couldn't decide whether to laugh with her or call emergency medical services. He helped her to the couch and refreshed her drink.

Man's Best Friend

Heerbo sat with tilted head at Meeroon's feet, studying her with great interest.

"I see it's a male," she observed with a smile.

Zoran struggled to hitch its pants on. "I'm in charge of thousands who jump when I tell them to, but I can't get Heerbo to poop on a toilet."

"Oh, my," she sniggered. "I'm curious. How did you come up with the name?"

"During an archeological dig, an old girlfriend found it alone inside a cave. I happened to be in the area and thought I'd observe. I could tell everyone was frustrated. No manner of enticement could get it to come out on its own. Don't know what I was thinking—it was supposed to be a joke of sorts, something I'd read about in the Earth historical archives, things the people said when they called their canine pets." Zoran shivered at the thought." *Should I really be saying this to a renowned journalist?*

Heerbo hummed at Meeroon's feet when she stroked its temples. "Yes?" she prodded.

"Don't know what made me do it, but I yelled out, 'Here boy.' Darned if it didn't come to me right away. Then, it wouldn't let go of me. After it cleared quarantine, Jaramana named it Heerbo and brought it here."

"Jaramana Caravodi?" she interrupted. "The project's archeological animal specialist?"

Uh oh. "Um—yes, that's her."

"I interviewed her yesterday. It'll broadcast in a couple days. Heerbo must be the discovery she mentioned. They originally thought the species had gone extinct. She must have trusted you to leave Heerbo in your care."

"Wasn't supposed to be permanent."

Electric tingles ran through his skin when she stopped petting Heerbo and touched Zoran's arm. The room suddenly warmed. Her perfume didn't help matters by instilling irresistible yearning.

Fur, *Feathers*, and Scales

"Like you." Heerbo mooned at her. "Stay."

"Heerbo, no," Zoran scolded. "Very impolite and inappropriate."

"Oh, he's fine," Meeroon said. "How could such an adorable creature consider a pleasant thought inappropriate?" She rubbed her nose on Heerbo's. "Can you go lie on the other couch while Zoree and Meeree talk to each other?"

Meeree?

Heerbo crawled to the coach, curled into a ball, and promptly fell asleep. How did these creatures manage to switch on and off like that at will, Zoran wondered?

"Heerbo seems to be rather taken with you," he said with mild surprise. "Pissed on my feet the day we first met."

"Jaramana called that behavior marking territory. As if to imply *you belong to me*," Meeroon said. "She claimed he's very perceptive. She is hopeful of finding another like him."

"That would be Jara, whose passion for indigenous animal welfare is exceeded by a disdain for her own kind."

Meeroon's eyes twinkled. "Her admiration of you now makes sense."

Admiration? Zoran thought it was Jara's way of getting back at him for cutting her budget.

Meeroon edged closer to him. "Perhaps they'll find a female."

The room temperature notched up extra degrees. "Infernal enviro system must be glitching." He made moves to fix it.

Meeroon gripped his arm to stop him. "Take your coat off."

Perspiration matted the back of his neck hairs when she helped slip it off his shoulders.

She batted eyelashes that had to be three centimeters long. "There, much better, don't you think?"

The surreptitious intention to refill his drink dashed, he sat back. She nuzzled closer. Every cell in Zoran's body vibrated to the essence of her fragrance wafting like a bubble around them.

He swallowed with a need to keep the conversation polite. "What else did Jara say about me?"

"That you, someone of your heritage index and multiple post-docs, chose against a comfortable position at home to go four light years away in hopes that we can return to the place of our origination. Her words were, 'Beneath the tireless passion for the reclamation of Earth lay a warm heart imprisoned by immense responsibility.' Quite poetic."

She ran a finger around his right ear and rubbed the soft skin behind it. "It takes a strong will not to let it change you, especially someone who hasn't been home in twelve years."

He took her free hand and got lost in the bottomless sea of her eyes. "Sometimes, it seems like a century, other times like I'd just arrived."

"I've been here a little under one Earth year. The seventy-day journey was boring, and I'm still adjusting to a diurnal cycle less than a tenth of ours back home.

"I'd define boring as the one hundred sixty years it took for our ancestors to make the journey to Salvuserit."

Heerbo grunted in his sleep and let out a sonorous fart that scaled three octaves.

Meeroon tucked her nose into Zoran's shoulder and giggled. Even the hypnotic power of her fragrance didn't stand a chance against the resultant reek. They found it difficult to plug nostrils while laughing.

Despite a freshened sinus awash with her perfume when the air cleared, a disturbing thought crossed his mind. "I'm still confused why Jara thought I'd be even remotely suitable to foster a mutant chimpanzee."

Amusement crinkled Meeroon's face. She pressed fingers against the tip of her nose. "Jaramana hasn't told you yet."

Fur, *Feathers,* and Scales

This can't be good. "Told me what?"

"Does Heerbo look like a monkey to you?"

As if timed, Heerbo rolled over and reached into his pants to scratch his butt.

"Never seen one before," he said. "Checked a few poorly restored archive pictures. Little tall for a chimp, maybe. Less hairy than I would have thought, which I assume to be from cave dwelling."

"Oh, my clueless darling," she tittered. "Heerbo is a human."

The shock of it stopped Zoran's breathing a moment. "That—looks nothing like a human," he huffed in a forceful exhale. "It lopes around on all fours most of the time."

"Thousands of years changes things, *Zordee,*" she ribbed. "We all had tails, lacked opposable thumbs, and *loped around* on four limbs at one time in our primordial past. Jaramana guessed regressional mutation and environmental influence were certainly factors, but Heerbo's genetic profile was indisputable."

"Why would Jara give me a *proto-human?*"

"Because he came to you; no one else. He sensed goodness in you." She sidled close and pressed herself against him. "Simple creatures instinctively sense a true friend. It can't be faked. They just know."

The spellbinding bouquet of her closeness swept through him like a solar flare. "It—he—seems to like you too."

"It proves we're compatible spirits." She snaked her hand beneath his shirt.

Zoran struggled to maintain civilized propriety. "I have to ask. Your perfume. It's driving me crazy."

"You *have* been away from home too long." She unbuttoned the top pin of his shirt. "You silly hound. I thought you high-index retriever types were the bright ones in our race. I'm not wearing perfume. I'm in estrus."

Man's Best Friend

She gently bit his ear with her canines. "Now enough talk of your pet human. Rub my belly."

Oranges and Roses

Angela Albertson
Winner, 2019 Short Story Award

Such simple creatures. They present themselves as smart, and I daresay that some even believe they are. They build roads as hard as rock and construct houses and buildings where no shelter was before. They deconstruct nature and design it to their will, and they've apparently even colonized the world. Whatever that means. They understand, or at least claim to understand, terms such as quantum mechanics, the laws of thermodynamics, and many other things that I am ignorant of. But, in so many other things, they lack the simple clarity with which we "lesser" beasts see the world. Free of stress from the mundane duties of being a productive member of society, we have plenty of time to simply be. I flap my lip and bend my neck back to look at the small girl beside me. She runs a soft brush over my short-coated body, sending specks of gray dust whisking into the air. "Do you know that you're half-witted, human?" I ask as she bustles about me.

She doesn't answer, of course. How could she? Humans have long since lost the ability to talk to animals. We were once the same. We were once kinfolk, but the people of the world craved knowledge and grew beyond us, and in doing so, lost the most important knowledge they ever had. I turn my head away from the girl and look down the barn.

A cool May breeze dances down the damp aisleway. It enters my nostrils, without asking permission for admittance, and travels into my lungs. The fragrance of earth and budding leaves swirl around me. The first blooms of the orange roses surrounding the barn add their own perfume to the air. Their bright scent has the smell of fruit and clover, like a warm summer's day.

I breathe in, inviting the air, saturated with fragrance, to enter my body. The afternoon rays of the sun stream in through the open barn doors. The old dog, lying in his usual spot, twitches his ear. He is spread out on a fuzzy, pilling blanket, and his jowl sucks in between his teeth before billowing outward with each noisy breath.

"Hey, Duke! Wake up!" I say to the hairy, yellow creature.

With a short inhalation of air, he sits up. "Huh? What'd I miss, Kit-Kat?"

"Nothing, really. Mostly smells. And I was just thinking about how senseless humans are."

Duke shakes his head. "You always do that. It's nothing to wake me up over. Have you ever given any thought to what a cynical little pony you are? Maybe try that for a change," he says as he flops back down on his mat with a soft thud.

I wiggle my head and let out an abrupt snort. "At least I'm intelligent."

The girl pauses in her constant fussing and fiddling with my hair and cocks her head at me. "Is there a fly that's bothering you?" she asks in her quiet, serene voice.

"No, Evie. I'm just talking to the dog. Carry on with my pampering."

Oranges and Roses

Evie walks up to my head and rubs the palm of her small hand on my forehead. "You know, I have something of a fly bugging me, too."

I peer around the girl to look at Duke. "See? Stupid. She's talking about insects, and I've already said I don't have one."

Duke sighs and rolls onto his back, letting his paws wiggle in the air.

The girl lets her hand slip off my face. "Mandy at school says that animals don't have feelings. That you can't love and that you can't care about me, either. Is that true?"

I take a step back to look at the child. My unshod hooves make a dull clop on the brick walkway as I inspect her. Her wide eyes stare at me, imploringly. One hand is shoved in the pocket of her pale pink jacket, and the other anxiously tugs at the cuff on her sleeve. I slowly shake my head back and forth, shimmying the locks of long, cream hair out of my eyes. I flare my nostrils and blow a cloud of air at her. Poor, naïve little thing. "You can just tell this Mandy-creature that she's the one without any feelings. Or brains," I say, bobbing my head to add enthusiasm to my answer. "Of course, we're capable of caring. If we weren't, why do you think we'd let humans do everything they do to us? Don't take this the wrong way, but I would certainly have trampled you by now if I didn't like you."

Evie sighs, letting her breath mingle with my own in the still, cool, spring air. She bows her head until her chin touches her slim chest. "I so wish you could answer," she whispers.

A pang of emotion weaves itself through my body. An unidentifiable sensation. I swivel my ears forward and back. Is this empathy? This dull ache that tugs at my chest like countless tiny hands are removing my pride and replacing it with sorrow? I lower my head and nudge her torso, brushing my nose against the slick fabric of her jacket. "But

Fur, *Feathers*, and Scales

I can! I'm telling you now. I just wish you were capable of hearing."

Duke sits up again. "She may not be able to hear our words, but she may be able to feel our warmth." He struggles his arthritic body upward and walks slowly toward her. He thrusts his cool nose into her hand and wags his tail.

She giggles. "Thanks, guys."

I lift my head and nuzzle her shoulder. I press my muzzle against her neck and breathe in her sweet scent of oranges and the faintest hint of roses. "Trust in yourself. You know the answer, even if no one else does. There will always be an impermeable divide between us, but that doesn't mean I am unable to care about you."

Duke backs a step away and swings his tail more vigorously. He barks. Once. I bump my muzzle against her still downturned head. "Don't let anyone tell you what to think. Follow what you know is right and never doubt it." I flick my lip against her soft cheek. "Look up and believe."

The girl raises her head and gazes into my eyes. She smiles. She reaches her hand out and places it on Duke's head. "I know you guys have feelings. I can see it."

Wolf King

Ralph Hieb

It was a late fall afternoon, and all the peaceful sounds of the Alaskan woods I had been enjoying for days were shattered by the howling of wolves, their voices raised in panic.

The prudent action would be to go in the opposite direction; instead, I was drawn toward them.

Walking with care, I approached the sound. It was coming from across a wide, frozen river. In the twilight, I could make out wolves standing on the far bank. Most had dark fur and blended in with their surroundings. Even with them semi-camouflaged, I could see that they stared at the frozen surface. After a moment of looking at the ice, I saw a hole in the surface, with a grown wolf struggling to escape the freezing water. It kept trying to toss something onto the ice.

With trepidation, I inched my way out onto the slick sheet. As I got closer to the wolf, I saw it was attempting to throw a pup from the water to safety. Still inching my way, I got closer until suddenly my footing gave way, and I found myself in the river. As I slid down, my arms reached up, and I felt something solid and small in my hands.

With the river only about ten or eleven feet deep, I hit the bottom and pushed up with all my might. My arms were stretched overhead, and the cold breeze of air told me they had reached the opening. The pup still in my hands, I threw it toward the waiting pack. My face breaking the surface, I was able to get a lungful of air before sliding under again. Having spotted the adult wolf close to me, it was apparent that it had given up, as it slid deeper into the water.

Drifting down, the adult wolf bumped into me. I pushed it above me and tried to throw it from the river, but the beast must have weighed well over one hundred pounds. With my breath exhausted, I shot to the surface, gulped some air, and then went under again, for the wolf. I grabbed it. This time with all my energy nearly expended, I launched myself upward. Its front legs slid onto the ice, then everything disappeared from my view. As the numbing water caressed me, I felt myself no longer freezing; a mild warmth settled on me. My fur parka was now too sodden to allow me the mobility to regain the surface. Reaching with my hands, I caught the edge of the ice and blacked out.

Regaining consciousness for only a moment, I felt the sleeves of the heavy parka being pulled, with me firmly zipped into it. I was being dragged over the frozen forest floor. I knew that my strength was exhausted, but took comfort knowing that the wolves would find me a tough meal.

Awakening in semi-darkness, I could tell it was early dawn or late dusk. A feeling of warmth surrounded me, along with the smell of wet fur. My parka was still damp but no longer freezing cold. Lying close and on top of me were the wolves. Moving my head slightly, I could see we were in a cave. Outside the cave entrance was the outline of a figure; I think it was watching me. It spread its arms, holding some kind of cloak, and disappeared. The only sound I heard was of a bird cawing; it was so loud I almost expected it to be in the cave with me.

Wolf King

My thirst was enormous. Trying to wiggle out from under the wolves would be a sure way to wake them, but I tried anyway. As I made my way out from under one wolf, another would move tighter against me. Giving up, I resigned to lie as still as possible.

Eventually, the animals on top of me moved so I could try to stand. The cave was only a few feet high, and the best I could do was to crawl on my hands and knees.

The wolves must have sensed that I was thirsty and hungry. Some of them used their noses to push me deeper into the cave. Although I should have been afraid, I sensed that they did not want to harm me. I soon got their meaning, and crawled further in and found a small pool of clear water. Falling next to it, I drank my fill. When I finished, they tried to push me back toward the spot I had been sleeping in. I must have fallen asleep, for a time.

When I awoke, with darkness slowly overtaking what light there was, a large wolf appeared and deposited a chunk of fresh meat in front of me. I was famished. Ignoring the wolves, I picked up the meat and started to tear into it with my teeth. I didn't think my teeth would be able to tear meat like I did, but I found little trouble ripping into my meal.

Even though I liked to have my meals cooked, I attacked this raw, and enjoyed it.

This went on for weeks. Soon, I grew comfortable in the presence of these creatures and stopped fearing them.

Looking out the end of the cave, I could see the days were growing shorter and colder, as darkness stretched further into the light. I crawled to the opening and looked at the surrounding woods. In the distance, I heard the river, along with various creatures of the night. The northern lights danced in the sky in swaths of green, white, and red or purple—colors I had never seen before in the night sky. The backdrop for them was a star-filled sky. The air was fresh with the crispness of new-fallen snow. I realized this was what I wanted when I set out on my journey: peace and quiet in the beauty of nature. No more people or their destructive ways.

Having no family or obligations to anyone, I decided to stay.

As the months progressed, my hair grew longer and instead of white, it had a silver shine to it. My strength seemed to increase, as did my eyesight and hearing. I didn't question what was happening, but decided to take it in stride.

The few times I went with the pack when they hunted, I knew I slowed them down. They tolerated my being there, but I had the uneasy feeling that they preferred I stay at the cave. I finally decided to remain behind and let them take care of me.

I stood next to the cave, enjoying the serenity of the night, when my thoughts were interrupted by a large, black wolf padding toward me. I had named him Butler, because he always showed up when I need something to eat, plus he had a white blaze on his chest, making it look like a tuxedo. Butler had a big piece of meat in his mouth that glistened with fresh blood.

As Butler approached, he dropped the meat in front of me and looked toward the ground. I was used to this method of receiving my meals. But this time, more of the pack gathered around, not one of them looking directly at me.

"What's up, Butler? How come everyone is around?"

From the corner of my eye, I noticed a man standing by a tree, watching me. When I looked directly at him, he ducked behind the tree, and the movement of a cape flowed with him. A moment later, I could hear the cawing of a raven as it flew into the high branches. It had to be the largest of its kind I had ever seen. Looking around, I saw that all the trees were filled with ravens. When the large one flew away, the rest followed.

Dropping the meat, I walked toward the tree. The sound of the wolves retreating made me turn and watch them. There was a dead caribou a short distance from the cave, and the pack had converged on it. I stayed back as the snarling and growling became furious. When I walked closer, they stopped and backed away from their meal.

"They will wait for you to finish before they feed again." It was the figure I had seen by the tree, and the branches were once again filled with ravens. I had been so interested in the wolves that I didn't hear the birds return.

By the sound of the voice, I could tell that what I thought to be a man was a woman, a woman with a voice that sang as she spoke.

"Who are you? And how do you know this?" I asked. The gruffness of my own voice startled me. It was a voice I had never heard before.

She answered, "You will know all when the time is right."

I looked at her and decided what I thought of as a cape was a black, shining gown. I watched her and wondered who she was and what she was.

She spread her arms wide, and the gown opened with the movement of her limbs into a pair of black, shining wings. Her body transformed into the large raven I had witnessed earlier. With a sudden flap of her wings, she was airborne and flew high over the trees. All the ravens followed, blocking the stars, making the sky dark. I stood still and watched until stars once again shone.

A noise broke my wonderment. Looking toward the pack, I saw that the wolves still held their positions. I walked back to the entrance of the cave. The sound of the

Fur, *Feathers,* and Scales

hungry pack tearing at the carcass resumed. I went inside and rested, trying to understand all that had happened.

The following day, a fresh layer of snow covered the ground. No trace of the caribou or any of the wolves was visible. Only the few that slept in the cave with me were still there, sound asleep. These wolves I thought of as my guard, but I didn't know what they were guarding us from.

Venturing outside of the cave, I felt a stillness over the land. Approaching the river, I saw tracks in the snow—the wolves were out hunting. I figured this meant that day I would have fresh raw meat again.

Wandering back to the cave, I realized I was beginning to enjoy the company of the wolves and their ways. They were far more organized than any human community I had ever been to. I laughed quietly to myself; this is now my family.

The sky became dark. Ravens in the thousands circled overhead. Then, the large one landed in front of me. The wings came down to her sides, and a second later, a woman stood before me.

"You need to call your wolves home," she said.

"What do you mean *my* wolves?" My stomach rumbled slightly at the thought of the fresh meat they would bring.

"You haven't figured it out yet."

I gave her a blank stare.

"They are your pack, your family. They consider you their alpha. That is why you can walk freely among them."

I had only recently thought of them as family. How could she see what I could not?

She raised her arms, and the wings appeared. With a great flap, she rose into the sky, followed by her loyal conspiracy of ravens.

Wolf King

I watched her fly away and wondered why I would be considered the alpha. Even more, I wondered why I needed to call the pack home. Where were they?

Listening as hard as I could, I heard no sounds from the wolves. Staring at the ground, I saw that their tracks were too jumbled to follow. When I inhaled deeply, in frustration, I could smell a hint of them.

Starting to run in the direction of the scent, I followed it across the completely frozen river. Continuing along the trail I had walked when I first heard the howls for help, straining to hear them, I continued to run, following the scent. As I ran, I started to wonder that the cold was not affecting me, and that my lungs didn't feel the exertion of my run.

When I finally found them, they had a woman and child trapped in a car, in the middle of a road. By this time, it was snowing again, and even with the snow piling up against the side of the car, a flat tire was visible, along with front-end damage. Several of the wolves that I normally saw were missing—ones I had given names to in my months of isolation with them in the cave. Sniffing the air, I sensed a metallic smell, a smell I now identified as dinner.

My attention was drawn back to the people in the car. The woman's eyes were glazed over as she observed me walk between the standing members of the pack. As I moved toward her, the wolves sat and looked at her. I came closer, watching her while she tried to shield her child from witnessing what I believed she thought was about to happen, me being killed by the pack.

The sound of howling came to me. I looked at the car and noticed, for the first time, blood smeared on it. She had hit an animal large enough to immobilize her vehicle.

Walking to the driver's window, I said in a loud voice, "Roll down the window, so we can talk."

Fur, *Feathers,* and Scales

She slid closer to the passenger side. Then, one of the larger wolves walked over and sat by the right-side window, his head halfway up the glass, staring at her. This caused her to slide to the center of the seat, while clutching her child.

I motioned with my hand to lower a window. Tentatively, she reached toward the door by me, and let the window come down, no more than an inch or two.

"Please don't hurt us." She was crying as she spoke.

"I won't hurt you and neither will the wolves." I wasn't completely sure about the latter part of my statement, but if I had to, I would step between them and her, while praying for the best. So far, not one of them showed any sign of aggression.

"Now, tell me what happened," I said.

"I hit a caribou. It ran away," she stammered.

"What are you doing out here?"

"I must have taken a wrong turn to my sister's house," she said.

I knew there was a road miles back that led to an ice road the natives use to get supplies and served as a short cut during winter.

A fresh howl told me the caribou didn't get far.

"You need to pop the trunk so I can change your tire." I tried to make my voice sound friendly, though I knew it now had a growl to it.

She reached for the lever by her seat, and the trunk lid lifted a few inches. I found what I needed to change the tire and got to work. The woman never got out of the car. The whole time she and her daughter clung to each other, watching me.

Afterward, I placed the tire and jack in her trunk. Closing it, I said, "You're all set."

"Who are you?" She spoke in a little above a whisper.

A smile was my reply.

Wolf King

She put the car in gear, and after her tires spun a little, it moved forward. She turned around and gave a timid wave, while watching the wolves.

It was several months later; the snow had melted and the first stalks of spring plants appeared. I was out for a stroll, enjoying the mild day, when the large raven appeared again.

"I have heard of your good deed," she said. "My ravens have told me that the people far off are saying that you are a guardian of the traveler." She cocked her head to the side. "Is this true?"

"I don't know what you are talking about," I said. "And how do your ravens speak to you?"

She ignored my question. "The woman you helped has said she would have been attacked by a pack of wolves if you had not arrived when you did. And that you fixed her vehicle and sent her away unscathed."

"I did what any decent person would do." I looked at all the ravens in the trees. They all started to squawk as if talking with each other.

"They are calling you the silver man." She laughed, then spreading her arms, she turned into a large raven again and flew away.

Her showing up unexpectedly and then disappearing was starting to annoy me. I still didn't know her name. I wondered what she meant by the silver man. She seemed to know a lot about everything in the woods, including me. Who was she?

My hearing was becoming more acute; I could hear my wolves from far away. But when howls rose on the wind, I didn't recognize any of the voices.

Deciding to investigate, I took off at a run toward them. I could hear my own pack following by my side.

Soon, I came upon an unfamiliar scene: Some of my pack had faced off with a pack of wolves I didn't recognize.

Neither pack moved toward the other. I assumed each was waiting for the other to make a move.

I don't know what possessed me, but I walked to the space between the two packs.

What I took to be their alpha cautiously crept toward me. He stared at me; I stared back, a challenge for superiority. Then to my surprise, he looked to the ground and rolled over, exposing his throat.

I approached him with caution. Kneeling by him, I gently rubbed his neck. When I stood, he rolled back and continued to look away from me.

The other pack crept closer. My pack still stood their ground, staring at me. I motioned for my pack to follow me as I walked back the way I had come. None of the strange pack moved to follow. As I moved along the trail, I could sense that they were no longer in my pack's hunting grounds. When I returned to my cave, wolves I had not seen before had joined the pack.

Once again, the sounds of ravens filled the air, as they flew in a large circle, then landed in the trees surrounding the cave.

The large raven landed in front of me and changed into her human form.

"Who are you?" I asked.

"Still you have not figured it out," she mocked. Shaking her head with a smile, she said, "I am Queen Raven. And I control all the ravens."

"In the world or just Alaska?"

Wolf King

"That is an excellent question. The truth is, I do not know." She looked around at her legion of followers. Without saying a word to them, they took to the sky as if rehearsed. "Now, Wolf King, it is time for you to meet the others who have become animal nobility. Please follow me."

She turned into her raven form and flew to join her flock.

I did not want to follow, but I wanted answers.

As she glided through the air, I ran, watching her. The ravens flapped their wings in a furious manner to keep pace, as she merely glided, occasionally moving her wings.

I wondered why she referred to me as a king. I knew that the wolves had a way of listening to my thoughts, and that I could run. I was never as fast as them, but they always slowed so that I could stay with them. Recently, my own strides seemed an easy gate, but when I looked to my side, I could see the pack was straining to keep pace with me.

My arms moved in perfect unison with my running. I was not winded, and when I looked down, watching the ground I covered, I was shocked. Instead of arms pumping the air, huge, silver, fur-covered legs kept reaching in front of me. And beating the ground were the largest wolf paws I had ever seen.

It is true. I am the Wolf King.

WHY BATS LIVE IN CAVES

Peter J Barbour
(Based on an African tale as told by
Stewart Matsopo of the Shona people)

There was a time, long ago, when Mother Nature forgot about the Namibian desert, an already parched part of southwest Africa. For a time, not even a little rain fell. It was so dry that the desert plants were dying, water holes were disappearing, and the animals were very thirsty.

When the animals became concerned for their survival, Lion, king of the beasts, consulted Elephant, respected for her wisdom; Great Eagle, most noble of birds, consulted Owl, wise, as owls were known to be.

"The birds and beasts should put aside their predatory habits and work together," Elephant and Owl said. "Together we could dig a well. We can divide the effort so that the beasts and birds work alternate weeks. The insects will help the beasts, and reptiles will help the birds."

The animals all agreed. The beasts worked the first week. Mongoose and Honey Badger burrowed in the dry sandy soil with nothing to quench their thirst. Rhino and Hippo moved the loosened soil with their huge noses. Butterflies and bees flew above the animals, flapping their wings and creating a breeze to keep the animals cool. As the beasts labored, Warthog discovered that Bat, instead of helping, rested in the shade by a rock. Warthog approached Bat.

"Brother Bat, why aren't you working?" Warthog inquired.

"I'm glad you asked," answered Bat. "It's not my week to work, Brother Warthog. So, as much as I would love to work with the beasts, I am not required. I'm not a beast."

"I thought you were a beast like us. You know, this is our week to labor," Warthog said with great pride.

Bat spread his wings and tilted his head. "You see, Brother Warthog, I have wings, and I can fly. Therefore, I'm not a beast. Do you know any other beasts that have wings and fly? I think not. As much as I would love to work with you, I don't have to. It's not my turn."

Warthog looked at Bat and scrunched up his eyes. He wondered if what Bat had told him was true, but he didn't pursue the discussion further. He simply returned to his task.

The next week, it was the birds' turn to work on the well. Flamingos and herons scratched at the ground; lizards and snakes scurried about breaking up clumps of grit. Storks and pelicans scooped up the dirt in their big bills and carried it away. Kingfisher saw Bat dozing while he basked in the sun. Kingfisher approached Bat.

"Brother Bat, wake up." Kingfisher nudged Bat with his pointed beak. "Why aren't you working?"

Bat stretched and yawned before he answered. "Can't you see I'm sleeping? As much as I would love to work with you, it's not my week to dig in the sand. It's the birds' turn. I am not a bird," Bat said as he unwrapped his wings from his body and showed Kingfisher that he lacked a beak and feathers. Kingfisher knit his brow, unsure whether Bat was telling the truth, but decided to return to his job.

Why Bats Live in Caves

The project continued for weeks. Bat rested when the beasts worked, claiming not to be a beast, and rested when the birds worked, claiming not to be a bird. After many weeks of hard labor, Meerkat struck water, and the well filled with the precious, life-sustaining liquid. All the animals stood around the well, pleased with themselves, ready to celebrate.

Tortoise, old and wise, came forward and addressed the animals. "I suggest that we commemorate this moment by having each animal say something about their experience digging the well."

The animals formed a large circle around the well, and each stepped forward to tell the others what role they performed to contribute to the project.

"I scooped out sand from the hole we created in the ground," said Giraffe as he held his head ever so high.

"I transported sand away from the well," said Guinea Hen in a deep, important voice.

But when it was Bat's turn to speak, he had nothing to say, because he had done nothing. Warthog brought this to the attention of Elephant; Kingfisher brought this to the attention of Owl. Elephant conferred with Lion, and Owl conferred with Great Eagle. Lion and Great Eagle asked Elephant and Owl to deliberate together and to advise them.

"Bat appears to be very lazy," Owl said to Elephant.

"He didn't work with the beasts, because he claimed to be a bird," said Elephant.

"He didn't work with the birds, because he claimed to be a beast," said Owl. "Well, what is he?"

Elephant and Owl went to Tortoise, who was neither beast nor fowl, and presented her with the facts.

"It is true," Tortoise began, "the bat has wings, and he can fly, but he lacks feathers and a beak, and doesn't lay eggs. Bats nurse their young, like all the beasts. I think Bat is a beast, not a bird."

Owl and Elephant brought Tortoise's conclusion to Lion and Great Eagle. Bat's laziness and his deceit pleased neither of them.

Lion and Great Eagle stood before the host of animals and decreed, "Bat worked with neither birds nor beasts. To punish Bat, we will make of him a hearty meal."

Bat heard this and feared for his life. *What can I do?* he thought. *I do not want to leave this place; it has the only water for miles around. If I fly away, surely, I will die of thirst. But if I stay here, the beasts and fowl will eat me. Where can I be safe?*

Bat hid under a rock, but the beasts found him there, and he took wing flying high above them. He could not fly forever, so Bat hid in a tree. When the birds found him there, he fled. Was nowhere safe for him?

He searched far and wide, but everywhere he went, there were either beasts or birds. Finally, he came to a cave. He flew deep inside. To fool the beasts, he clung to the cave's ceiling well out of their reach; to fool the birds, he came out only at night when most everyone else was asleep. And ever since that day, that has become the way of bats.

Goats in the Machine

Christopher D. Ochs

Erwin kicked his clodhoppers into the corner of the mudroom, hard enough to topple over the herd of brooms huddled there. Stomping sock-footed into the kitchen, he roared, "I swear your lunkhead nephew is out to bankrupt the farm."

Florence set a steaming pot of mashed turnips on the table, next to a gravy boat brimming with melted cheese sauce. A shake of her head sent her graying ponytail wagging. "Oh, dear. What did Neil do this time? Mix the seed with the animal feed again?"

"He'd better not. I posted the county agent's signs on the granary bins yesterday. Not even he could miss 'em now." Erwin exchanged his Mudhens cap for the handkerchief in his coveralls' back pocket and wiped the sweat from the front of his brow back to his growing bald spot. Yanking a bottle of water from the refrigerator, he emptied half of it before resuming his rant. "That durn fool was supposed to take the tractor and turn over the spring onion field. He ran four rows before he realized he didn't properly attach the plow trailer. After wasting the first half of the morning, then he sets the rack to the wrong depth, and breaks the quick-release hitch on deep fieldstone. It's gonna take me all of tomorrow to repair the hitch and realign half the blades."

Florence squinted out the window next to the oven, shielding her eyes against the setting sun. "Which means the spring cauliflower is going to sit in the field another day past its harvest time. Hope it don't over-ripen and go to seed."

"I swear, if he weren't family, I'd—"

"One more month, dear, 'til he finishes his internship and heads back to Texas A&M. Besides, how many times did you say you needed the help?" Florence thumped a platter holding a small roast on the table with enough force to make the pot of turnips rattle on its trivet. "Now, you shush. Neil's coming up the lane. And he looks quite upset."

Neil burst in, skidding to a halt in the mudroom. He bent over, hands on knees, and his chest heaving for air in spasms.

"What did you break this time?" said Erwin, slamming the water bottle back into the fridge and bracing himself for the inevitable bad news.

"Goats got out. . . . Loose in . . . wheat field." Earbuds hanging from his neck swung in rhythm with each gasp.

"How on earth?" blurted Florence. "I *know* I locked their pen after milking time."

"Oh, great," said Erwin, slapping his cap back on, and jamming on his boots still untied. "They can tear up a field faster than you can spit. How much did they wreck, Neil?"

Neil jerked his thumb toward the outside door. "You gotta . . . see this," he wheezed with an incredulous grin.

Erwin stomped out of the house. Florence tossed her oven mitts on the table before jogging after her husband. Neil puffed along behind, his right hand pressed against his side, nursing a growing side-sticker. The three of them dashed past the immense Quonset hut filled with farm machinery in various states of repair, rounding the low hillock that separated the scraggly back yard from the fields. Once they got to the wall of fieldstone separating the plots of winter wheat from alfalfa, Erwin spouted his choicest selection of profanities.

A thin, straight-line path of flattened stalks rolled from the open metal gate into the heart of the field. Deep in the center of the wheat, a dozen goats' heads bobbed up and down, disappearing behind the tall grain. They bleated happily as they munched away.

Erwin was about to storm headlong toward the wayward flock when both voices behind him cried out.

"Wait, Unka Erv. Take a look first," puffed Neil.

Erwin wheeled around and scowled at him, before regarding his wife with a slightly less annoyed frown. She stood on the middle rail of the gate, her palm shielding her eyes against the beet-red sun as she peered over his head.

"You may want to look before you leap, dear."

"Whaddya mean?" Erwin joined Florence on the rail and followed her gaze.

The goats gathered in four areas: a central open expanse wide as an 18-wheeler, surrounded by three smaller, round, bare patches. Each clearing was leveled, the grain either trampled down or chewed up. A handful of contented animals trotted back and forth between the ruined areas.

"So, what's to see," Erwin demanded, "other than money down the drain?"

"Look closer, dear." said Florence, with the patient tone she reserved to nudge Erwin on those occasions when he missed the forest, the trees, and the sequoia about to fall on him.

After sighing out a long breath of exasperation, he squinted under the shadow of his cap's brim. Surveying the scene again, Erwin straightened his spine, and his shoulders shivered. He uttered a subdued, "Oh."

He dropped his hand and spat in the direction of four perfectly circular areas, connected by paths straight as lasers. "You gotta be kiddin' me. Crop circles?"

Erwin and Florence stepped off the gate. Florence shot Erwin a look that told him to maintain something that approached a cool temper before she jogged back to the barn.

It didn't work. "What kind of lame-brain stunt is this?" bellowed Erwin.

"Honest, Unka Erv," pleaded Neil. "I been sprayin' the soybeans in the north field all afternoon and was bringin' the tank and sprayer back to the equipment shed." His arm swept from the north to the farmhouse, his hand pointing to the herringbone tire treads in the dirt road paralleling the stone wall. "When I spotted the goats and the weird pattern, I gunned the tractor fast as it would go."

A chain of rapid barks sounded from the barn and grew in volume and exuberance as they approached. On legs flailing so fast they were rendered a blur, a furry ball of black and white rounded the far corner of the stone wall. Florence coughed as she faded behind the storm of dust and dirt the galloping border collie had kicked up.

Erwin curled his lower lip between his teeth and piped a triplet of whistles that made Neil wince. "Good girl, Bear. Round 'em up." He pointed an arm into the field and whistled again, while Neil crammed his hands against his ears.

The hefty dog zoomed to the gate, only to skid to a dust-clouded stop at the first row of wheat. Her bushy tail curled under her haunches, and she shimmied back, a tremulous whimper replacing her series of yaps.

"What's the matter, Bear?" Erwin wheedled the whining ball of quaking fur. Stabbing his arm at the heart of the wheat field, he coaxed the border collie with trumped-up enthusiasm. "Get 'em, girl." The dog curled up tighter, shivering like a thunderbolt had struck.

Goats in the Machine

Erwin stomped into the field, following the lane of flattened wheat. When he entered the central area, the various small herds of goats abandoned the outer circles to join him.

"You can't herd goats by yourself," said Neil through cupped hands. "Even I know that."

"Some days you can't, some days you can. If I can get the Billy to help," Erwin called over his shoulder. "or if I can corner the new kid, his nanny might get the rest of the flock to follow."

He faced the herd again to find thirteen bleating heads circled around him. They stared at him with blank expressions while chewing mouthfuls of grain. Erwin plowed past the nannies, heading toward the Billy, who waggled his horns. He found his way blocked by another goat. Snatching a fistful of trampled grain stalks, he flanked the animals, searching for the young goat kidded last week. Once more he was stymied by a doe that meandered into his path. After a few more attempts separated by as many curses, Erwin found himself at the entrance of the main circle, surrounded by a tight formation of nannies.

Holding out the stalks, he cajoled them with a mild voice, "Okay, if you want to play follow the leader, I'm game." Stepping backward through the gate, Erwin beamed with satisfaction as he led the entire trip of goats back to their pen. Latching their gate, he tossed the crumpled stalks at the animals and declared to Florence with a thumb under one overall strap, "There, it's easy to outfox 'em."

"I don't know, dear," said Florence, her eyebrows cocked with well-practiced sauciness. "More like they herded *you* out of the field."

They ate their lukewarm dinner of roast, turnips, and greens topped with Florence's fresh cheese 'n' horseradish sauce in fragile silence, broken by sparse comments about the weather or the food. Erwin ruminated over his turnips, and Florence suppressed a snicker at how her husband's sideways chewing resembled that of the herd's Billy. Whenever Neil tried to bring up a topic anywhere near the broken hitch or the goats, Erwin silenced him with a glower that threatened to char the heel of the roast.

Erwin pulled the napkin from his shirt and flung it on his plate, ending the meal. With a stern flick of his brow at Neil, he screwed on his Mudhens cap. "I'm gonna get a head start on repairing that hitch, before hitting the hay. And Neil, you take the harvester into that winter wheat field at crack-o'-dawn before the goats get in there again."

After hours of elbow grease, Erwin managed to get the hitch welded back, but a pair of plow-boards remained off kilter. The racket he raised from realigning them was interrupted when Florence cut the power to the equipment shed—her subtle hint that she needed sleep.

Erwin's night, however, was fitful at best. The worries and frustration about Neil's incessant incompetence, the goats' curious behavior, and the farm's general state of (dis)repair made sleep elusive. His single parcel of blissful slumber was interrupted with a snort and a hack when Florence shook him awake in the predawn light.

She pulled up a pair of jeans under her nightgown as she peered through an open window. "Do you hear that? Sounds like the goats are out in the fields again." Exchanging a flannel shirt for her gown, she continued to crane her neck, tilting her head with a squint that compressed her face into a mass of wrinkles. "And there's something strange out there, too. I can barely make out the tops of whatever it is."

After a string of incoherent grumbles, Erwin threw on a pair of coveralls and a shirt. Tromping past Neil's door, he pounded once on the wall. "Wake up. You're supposed to be in that wheat field by now." The second he tied on his boots, Erwin clomped out of the house like a field marshal to

Goats in the Machine

war. Florence and a bleary-eyed Neil trailed behind. Their full head of steam staggered to a disjointed stop once they rounded the hillock.

Outlined by a pink sunrise far less ready for the new day than Neil towered a dozen stone pylons, each taller than a man. Composed of large fieldstones fitted tighter than a jigsaw puzzle, they stood arranged in a perfect circle spanning several otherwise undisturbed rows of knee-high alfalfa.

Florence tapped Erwin on the shoulder, pointing toward the wheat field. Her husband could do nothing except cock his head and blink in wonder at the remains of the ravaged fieldstone wall. A breeze whistled past the gaping holes and ragged rubble of shattered mortar, and the metal gate fell over with a resounding clang, its anchor of stone having been removed.

From the center of the henge trumpeted a bleat, though to Florence's ears it sounded more like the warbling of an operatic soprano. Lasting a full five seconds, it grabbed the trio's attention more strongly than that of a crying child.

From behind each pylon popped up a goat's head, contentedly munching a mouthful of alfalfa. In unison, they all bleated a vigorous response. Just as swiftly, they all fell silent, leaving only the sound of wind rustling the rows of greenery.

One by one, out of the field the errant goats marched. First emerged the recently foaled kid. Unusually shaggy for such a young buck, he pranced out from the stalks between the nearest pylons. One by one, eleven Nannies followed in lock step, trailed closely by the lone Billy. The slotted irises of their eyes never wavered as they walked in stately procession along the crumbling shambles of the fieldstone wall, not once maa-ing a single cry at the gawking farmers.

Erwin and the others followed in stunned silence behind the goats. The unlikely parade ended with the kid turning around in the center of their farm pen. He screamed another of his seconds-long bleats. The goats filled the pen, with the Billy grabbing the chain between his teeth and pulling the enclosure gate closed behind him.

"Now, there's something you don't see every day," said Neil.

Florence faced her husband. Her widening eyes darted between the goats and the far-off circle of stone. "Dear, we've got to contact someone. The police, the county farm agent, or maybe..."

"Now, don't go all Mulder and Scully on me, woman," Erwin groused.

"Well then, what do *you* suggest we do?"

"You know what this is?" said Erwin with a resolute snap of his fingers. "This smells like one of Pratchett's pranks."

"You can't be serious, Erwin," Florence sputtered.

Neil scratched his head. "Who's Pratchett?"

"Our goofball neighbor," said Erwin with a widening frown. "He's always pulling stunts like this. He ain't satisfied with having the biggest pumpkin in the state, or his high 'n' mighty prize-winning corn. He's probably cheesed off because the county agent selected our farm to test that new-fangled company's corn seed."

"This doesn't feel like a prank, dear," said Florence as she scratched her chin. "I mean, look at poor Bear." The doghouse by the side of the house rattled, and a ragged whine spilled out of its front opening.

Erwin whipped the cap off his brow and slapped the road's dust from his coveralls. "You call whoever you want, Flo. The veterinarian, the county agent, or MIB for all I care. But don't come cryin' to me when the nice men in white coats come to fit you for a straitjacket. In the meantime, I got a farm to keep from goin' under." He corralled Neil by the shoulder and herded him toward the equipment shed. "Take the harvester and bale up that wheat field—crop circle nonsense and all. I'm gonna finish fixin' the plow rack, so's I can plant that new corn."

Florence planted fists on hips, shaking her head as the men trudged away. Without a word, she surrendered to her own daily cycle of chores and tending to the diminishing numbers of the farm's livestock: feeding the chickens and gathering their eggs, slopping the two remaining hogs, and lastly, milking the goats and prepping the milk to make cheese.

Three things made her chuckle while she made her appointed rounds this day. Anticipating the princely sums the rounds of her *chevre* goat cheese fetched at the farmers' market was one—it amazed Florence what was run of the mill ten years ago was considered "artisan" today. The second was hearing the thump of a hammer, hitting something it shouldn't, coming from the equipment shed, followed by Erwin's bellow of a novel combination of expletives. Last on the list was the way the extraordinarily shaggy kid behaved around her.

Most other goat kids Florence had raised suckled as soon as they could walk. Otherwise, when not orbiting their mothers for a meal, they would buck and bounce with abundant life, play-butting anything that moved, or attempting to climb anything that didn't. But this hairy, little buck was content to stand and watch, silent and unblinking, as the two-legged intruder milked the nannies. Florence's chuckle degraded to a quiver in her gut when the thought occurred of the kid letting loose with another of his seconds-long screams.

She poured the last of the day's milk into the curding vessel, along with the rest of that week's collection and a heaping dollop of starter culture from the barn's cooler. Scrutinizing the tubful of milk with a dubious eye, she was distracted by its curious tinge of azure. Like last week's batch, it reminded her of the bluish liquid concoction that powdered milk would produce. "Well," she convinced herself with a shrug, "last night's sauce tasted just fine to me."

Florence was interrupted by the approach of an unfamiliar engine and the crunch of gravel. Emerging from the barn, she spotted a dilapidated sedan with municipal plates coming to a halt, straddling one of the deeper ruts in their long driveway. Out popped a wiry man with an impeccably straight comb-over and horn-rimmed glasses. Concern and worry were written in the set of his jaw. Spotting Florence, he marched over to her with determination in his step and clipboard in hand.

"Good morning, Mrs.—"

"Call me Florence," she said with an inquisitive smile as she toweled off smears of starter from her hands.

"Pleased," he replied with a half-hearted handshake. "I'm Mr. Chambers, with the county branch of the Farm Service Agency. I've spoken with your husband on several occasions. Is he about?"

Another thump and string of rude words trumpeted from the Quonset hut. "That would be him now," said Florence with an embarrassed roll of her eyes. Leading Chambers over, curiosity got the better of her. "Is there a problem?"

"There's been a slight mix-up in seed distribution. I hope we caught it in time. But first, if you don't mind me asking . . ." Chambers dawdled with a quizzical glance over his shoulder. "What's that new construction in your alfalfa field?"

Florence replied with a nervous titter. "That's somebody's idea of a joke. We discovered it only this morning. My husband and I were talking it over an hour ago, about who to call. So, it's just as well you're here. He thinks our neighbor pulled an elaborate prank, but I don't know . . ."

Goats in the Machine

They strolled past Neil, who had successfully hitched the harvester, but was currently waist deep under the tractor's hood while he tinkered with the engine. Passing from the bright morning sun into the comparative gloom of the shed, Florence called out, "Dear, the county agent, Mr. Chambers, is here to see you."

An exasperated sigh and a clatter of tools echoed from behind two tractors, one gutted for parts. Erwin emerged from the machinery, wiping his blackened hands on a rag. "The Farm Service? What's up this time, Chambers? Did I forget to dot an i or cross a t?"

Chambers batted Erwin's arrogance away with a wave of his hand. "No, not at all. The mix-up's on our end this time, I'm afraid." He flipped a body of papers over the top of his clipboard. "More precisely, the fault is on the part of the distributor. You were sent the wrong batch of corn for seed." Chambers peered over his glasses. "We were hoping you didn't plant it yet. The manufacturer is quite anxious to get it back. Of course, they'll exchange it for the correct load of experimental seed tomorrow." He pinched out an apologetic smile, like his face muscles were unaccustomed to the work. "Free of charge, of course."

Erwin tried to set his shoulders in a façade of boiling anger, but he could only percolate out one of annoyance. He nodded his head in the direction of the piles of discombobulated metal behind him. "You're in luck. The plow's broken, and we haven't had a chance to clear the field for planting." Erwin tossed the oily rag on the nearest tractor wheel and led the pair outside to the granaries beyond the far side of the barn. "Over here, in bin number three."

"Three? But . . ." Florence's eyebrows danced like a broken seesaw. She bit her lip and followed the two men.

Erwin came to a sudden halt in front of the second bin's chute. With a growl, he glared at the sign beside the chute and tore it off. "What the . . . Did you change this back, after

Neil's screwup?" He thrust the obnoxiously bright, plastic sign labeled "GenGrain C-427" at his wife, who could only reply with a shrug of her shoulders and a shake of her head. He flipped up the gate at end of the chute, and coarse millet poured around his boots. Erwin's chest inflated like a hot air balloon. "Neil," he shouted, loud enough to be heard in the next county. His nephew trotted over with an expression of utter innocence, which only infuriated Erwin to the point where his neck flushed bright as a freshly painted fireplug.

Erwin waved the sign in front of Neil's nose, close enough to nearly slice it off. "I put this up so you didn't mix up the grains again. Why did you change it back?"

"Honest, Unka Erv, I haven't touched it."

Erwin threw the sign on the ground and glowered at his wife. "Well, the *goats* sure as hell didn't do it."

"The way the past few days have been going, they just might've." Florence muttered under her breath.

A light turned on behind Erwin's eyes, and he clapped his hands together. "I knew it! I *told* you Pratchett's been up to no good."

"What seems to be the problem?" said Chambers, adjusting his glasses that had vibrated down his nose. "And where's my corn?"

Florence stepped past Chambers to face her husband. "If this is the grain mix-up you mentioned yesterday, then I've been feeding it to the goats for the past month."

Erwin flashed a look of shocked disbelief at his wife.

"*Fed?*" he and Chambers cried out in unison.

Erwin slid up the gate on the third chute. Hardened maize veined with a curious tint of azure spilled onto the ground.

All the blood drained from Chambers' face. "Oh, good grief. This is a worst-case scenario. That's GenGrain's latest GMO product. It hasn't been cleared for open field tests. It's not even supposed to be outside the lab yet. And it's certainly not to be *fed* to anything."

The gravel around their feet began to vibrate, and a strange rumbling grew into a fever-pitched whine akin to that of a screaming jet.

"Where in tarnation is that coming from?" Erwin hunkered down the visor of his Mudhens cap to shield against the morning sun as he turreted his head, searching for the source of the deafening clamor.

The ground shivered, growing in strength until it quaked. All four of them struggled to maintain their balance. The ribbed, metal sheets of the Quonset hut exterior rattled, then screeched in agony. Their rivets popped off, and the metal skin of the equipment shed tore away, revealing a tornado building in size and speed. Erwin and the others ducked, expecting rivets and shrapnel to pepper them and the surrounding ground. When they ventured to raise their heads again, they spied the rivets being drawn back into the howling column of swirling debris of tools, tractor parts, and splintered building.

With a strange, zipping sound, the metal plates dove one by one into the heart of the maelstrom, disappearing into a strange blue light that pulsed in the crumbling remnants of the equipment shed. Beams, rivets, engine parts, and Plexiglas windows followed suit, sucked into the heart of the spinning chaos in rapid succession.

In the space between heartbeats, the whirling dervish of metal and plastic came to a silent, mid-air halt. Illuminated from the unearthly blue glow within, the remaining flotsam fell to the ground with a crashing roar surpassing that of a train wreck. Above the settling debris rose a craft roughly shaped like a disc. From its bottom emanated an intense blue that the eye refused to focus on. The central rim of the disc was lined with portals of Plexiglas, bent and fused to the ribbed metal that once formed the exterior of the Quonset hut.

Through each window peered a goat. In the window directly facing the humans was the shaggy kid. Staring at Florence with a tilt of his head and a silent bleat that came uncomfortably close to a smile, the young buck raised one of his fore hooves—and waved.

The blue light pulsed violently, and the disc rose with a hum that made Florence's bones itch, until it vanished into the blinding sun.

The four of them stood in a daze until they paced, slow as sleepwalkers, in the direction of the demolished Quonset hut.

"What just happened?" Erwin squeaked like a child about to cry.

Florence thrashed her head to settle her wits back into place. Halting in front of Chambers, she grabbed him by the shoulders. "What was in that GMO grain? What have I been feeding our goats?"

"I don't know," replied Chambers. He fumbled with his clipboard, then let it fall from his grip. "I have a feeling if GenGrain told us, they'd have to kill us."

"I don't understand," whined Erwin.

"You just might, dear. And sooner than you'd expect," Florence said, followed by an unnerved swallow. "The goats have been eating that corn for a month, and we've been eating their cheese for the past several weeks."

Bease

Will Wright

I rarely criticized Bease's taste in girls. Claudia was gorgeous, and unlike many beautiful girls, she never had an unkind word for anybody. Maybe that's why Bease hoped she'd go out with him. Most of the girls in our school kept their distance from Bease. One told me she wouldn't spit on Bease 'cause he might think she was trying to kiss him. Though awkward, and perpetually lovesick, Bease remained irrepressibly hopeful.

Bease's real name was Thomas. He'd been Bease since second grade when Jeremy Del Clate noticed that his scrunched-up features and thick glasses made him look a little like Mrs. Beasley, the doll that the little girl, Buffy, carried on the show *Family Affair*.

Nine years later, only his mother and Principal Pappel called him Thomas. Once I heard his Mom slip and call him Bease. If the name bothered him, he didn't show it. All Bease seemed to care about was finding a girlfriend. He'd been that way back before most guys even wanted girls around.

"Claudia is nice," said Bease.

"That's true," I said. It was my policy to be honest with Bease. If he asked me if Claudia would go out with him, I'd tell him no, but I couldn't deny that she seemed like a nice person.

"And she doesn't have a boyfriend," he added.

"That's true, too," I said. As a matter of fact, I'd never seen Claudia with any guy. She didn't seem to be into girls either. She was always there, looking gorgeous, pleasant to all who spoke to her, but almost always alone.

I don't know about the other guys, but the reason I stayed clear of Claudia was because I found her intimidating. Any girl that nice and that good-looking was too good for me. I wondered if she was alone because other guys felt the same way.

"I think she's lonely," said Bease.

"Could be," I admitted, though it hadn't occurred to me until that moment.

"She's like me," said Bease.

"She likes you?"

"No, she is like me."

"Bease," I said, "how in the world is Claudia Diamente like you?"

"Well, we're both lonely."

"Bease, buddy, you're doing it again. You're setting yourself up for another heartbreak. Claudia will not go out with you."

"Why not?"

"Because she's gorgeous!"

"And she's lonely—like me."

I might as well have saved my breath. Once Bease got it into his mind that a girl might like him, nothing stopped him short of crushing rejection. I'd been there to watch the inevitable disaster enough times to know; girls at school, girls in the neighborhood, the lifeguard at the pool, the girl at the pet shop.

Bease had a cage full of canaries from the summer he pursued Kaitlin from the pet shop. Kaitlin, two years older

Bease

and a bird lover, was friendly to Bease longer than any other crush, largely because she couldn't believe that such a pathetic guy had any hope that she might be interested.

Hope was a commodity Bease had in abundance. Perhaps he had so much hope that there was no room left for common sense. I mean, he still wrote letters for heaven's sake, but he only got one written reply. It was a stern letter from Emma Watson's agent telling him that Ms. Watson was in a committed relationship and asking him to please stop sending her lyrics to love songs he had written.

Bease showed me one of his songs. It was predictably awkward, but I give him credit for finding so many phrases that rhyme with Hermione.

You had to figure with so many crushes that several of them must have overlapped. Could a guy be madly in love with two or three girls at the same time? For all his social failings, Bease had more capacity for love than any other guy I knew.

And that's how he was until one Sunday when he got involved with a female that was happy to love him back.

Her name was Stargirl; at least that was her name after Bease named her. Stargirl was a stray cat that must have lived with people sometime because when Bease called to her, she ambled right up to him. Stargirl was a gray tabby with a torn ear, two-thirds of a tail, and a sore on her side that didn't look good at all.

It didn't smell good either, or maybe that was Stargirl's natural scent.

"Really, Bease?" I asked as he picked up the putrid cat.

"She likes me!"

"She'd like you to feed her."

Bease held the cat toward me. Stargirl hissed. "No," said Bease, "it's me. She likes me."

A smelly half-hour later, the cat was still attached to Bease even though he hadn't fed her anything.

Fur, Feathers, and Scales

"All right," I agreed. "She likes you, but she's still an ugly, stinky cat. You should take her to a shelter."

"They'd kill her in the shelter!"

"They might be doing her a favor."

"Don't say that."

"You can't keep her, you know. You've got a cage full of canaries, and isn't your Mom allergic to cats?"

"Yeah," said Bease, rubbing his face into the cat's putrid coat. "Hey! We can keep her at your house!"

"No, Bease. I'm not having that stinky cat anywhere near where I eat or sleep or . . . brush my teeth."

"Well, I can't just let her go."

"Why not?" I asked. "She was on her own until today; she'll be fine. Cat's do great in the wild."

"Not this one," said Bease as he pulled out the tail of his shirt to wipe the puss off the cat's smelly wound.

"Look—the cat doesn't even like me. Even if I was willing to keep her, she'd just run away." Stargirl gave me a look that I'm pretty sure was the cat equivalent to *Up yours, Fella*.

"Aw," said Bease. "There's just gotta be a way."

You'd think somebody who'd been told, "No way," by so many girls would stop believing that there had to be a way. I breathed a little easier. The last thing I wanted at my house was a typhoid feline that hated my guts. If I wanted someone around who hated me, I could ask Mr. Learishaw, the gym teacher, to live at my house. He'd probably hang a rope from my basketball hoop just to make me climb it all the time.

"Claudia," said Bease.

"She won't go out with you, dude."

"Maybe not, but she's the answer."

"What's the question?"

"I'll give Stargirl to Claudia! Stargirl will have a good home, and Claudia will love me!"

Bease

I know it was cruel, but I couldn't help it. I laughed. "Bease, please! Think for a minute."

"That's the answer," said Bease. He must have been talking to himself because he was ignoring me, lost in his hopeful fantasy.

"Bease, are you hearing me? Claudia is not going to want a diseased stray! She's going to think you're weird or sick, maybe both."

"I'll do it at school tomorrow!"

"Bease, you can't bring a cat to school! At least not unless it's dead and soaked in formaldehyde, which," I sniffed at Stargirl and nearly got a claw across my face, "this cat almost qualifies. But you don't want to give the girl you like an animal to dissect in Bio. Nobody does that, Bease!"

"I just need a place to put you for one night," he said to the cat as she licked his nose.

Then both Bease and the cat looked at me. I swear, they did it together like some grotesque dance routine. One moment they were staring into each other's eyes, and then they moved in unison to point four eyeballs at me. For one eerie moment, they looked related.

"No, man! I told you. I don't want a cat in my house! I don't like this cat. I don't like the way she smells. I don't even like healthy cats that aren't trying to scratch my eyes out. There is no way I'm running a hotel for diseased hell cats."

I was as firm as I knew how to be. That's why two hours later I was moving boxes and junk in the basement.

I'm not sure if it was the sound of moving boxes or the yowling and hissing that brought Mom down.

"What is going on down here?"

I was doing my best to corral Stargirl into a corner. I didn't want her wandering around all night. Cats, I was learning, were not easy to contain.

"Is that a cat?" asked Mom.

"Yeah," I said, "but it might also be an evil zombie."
"What is he doing here?"
"She, actually. Mom meet Stargirl."
"You got a cat without asking? You don't even like cats!"
"I don't want her, Mom. Bease picked her up from the street. He's going to give her to a girl at school."
"Oh. . . . Surely not."
"That's his plan."
Mom stared at Stargirl, taking in her numerous deficiencies. "Your friend," she said at last. "It just breaks your heart."

I suppose it's possible that Mom's heart was breaking for Stargirl, but I think it was more likely for Bease, who never seemed to find a reasonable way of showing his affection for girls. Nevertheless, Mom applied her considerable compassion on the stinky hell cat, cleaning her wound, combing her fur, making every effort to make Stargirl less hideous.

For her part, Stargirl didn't hiss at Mom or try to scratch her as she did with me. Maybe the can of tuna had something to do with that.

Bease was jumping up and down when I answered the door next morning. He didn't need to pee; he was excited.

"Where is she?"
"Down in the basement."
"She didn't sleep with you?"

I didn't have to answer. Bease was already bounding down the basement stairs. I heard Stargirl make a hideous sound that might have been hell cat for *Where have you been?* Moments later Bease was running back up the stairs with Stargirl mounted triumphantly on his shoulder.

Even after all of Mom's work the night before, the cat looked disgusting, but she was a happy disgusting, that was clear. She and Bease had made a connection. I shook my head. There was no way this was going to end well.

Bease

We ended up walking to school because even Bease recognized that Grundy the bus driver wouldn't let Stargirl on her bus.

Jeremy Del Clate, the top jock in our school and the class Romeo, pulled over his Mercedes convertible when he saw us. In many ways, Jeremy, who had given Bease his nickname, was the anti-Bease. Girls swooned over him. Freshman year, he had taken three dates to the same dance, and none of them complained.

I hated him. I don't know how Bease felt. Jeremy was always a jerk to him, but Bease's focus never strayed from the current girl of his dreams. I wasn't even sure he noticed Jeremy.

Maybe that's why Jeremy was such an ass with Bease. Jeremy didn't like being ignored.

"What's that on your shoulder, Bease," he asked, "VD of the esophagus?" Not content to hurl an insult and drive on, Jeremy slowed his German status symbol to our walking pace.

"This is Stargirl," said Bease. "I found her yesterday."

"How, was it clogging your plumbing?"

"No," said Bease, looking unannoyed and still walking purposely toward school. "She just walked up to me."

"So, you're putting her back?"

"No, we're bringing her to school."

Jeremy shot me a look of amused contempt. Unlike Bease, I was not immune to scorn. It was so unfair. I wasn't bringing Stargirl to school. I was just there for moral support. But if I said that in front of Bease, that wouldn't have been very supportive, so I just kept my mouth shut and tried to think of at least one snappy comeback I could hurl at Jeremy.

"Hey, Bease," said Jeremy. "I think the roadkill is supposed to be dead before you dissect it."

Fur, *Feathers*, and Scales

All right, I felt a little ashamed there. I had had almost the same thought the day before, and as embarrassing as it was being Bease's best friend, there was no way I wanted to be like Jeremy!

Half a mile from the school parking lot, Jeremy finally pulled away. "He's probably gone to make trouble for you, Bease," I said. "You're really not supposed to bring pets to school."

"I'm just bringing Stargirl to Claudia."

"And what if Claudia doesn't want her?"

Stargirl's head, previously resting on Bease's chest as she rode his shoulder, rose up to look Bease in the eye. "How could Claudia not want her?" he asked.

I had a lot of answers to that question, but I knew Bease, and my answers wouldn't mean a thing to him—if he even heard them. I was there for moral support. Bease wasn't looking for advice.

By the time we got to school, Jeremy had raised a small welcoming committee. Nine or ten guys, mostly jocks, gave us a mock cheer as we walked onto the grounds.

"Is that your girlfriend, Bease?" asked Jordan Strong.

"Maybe it's his sister," said a kid I didn't know.

Just as Bease was deaf to unwanted advice, he seemed not to hear abuse either. He looked happy and proud as he marched through the gauntlet, up the steps, and into the school. With Stargirl firmly attached to his shoulder, he walked by the school office as if he had nothing to hide. If it had been me, vice principals would have streamed out of the office, zip-tied my arms and legs, and carried me off to permanent detention.

With Bease, nobody said a word. I was wondering what the homeroom teacher would say, when Claudia came around the corner.

"Hey, Claudia!" said Bease.

"Hello, Bease," said Claudia.

Bease

"What?" said Jeremy, who I hadn't realized was right behind me. "Is he hitting on Claudia now? Nobody's good enough for her!"

"She turn you down, Jeremy?"

"I caught her on a bad day."

Claudia was still talking to Bease, but I couldn't hear what they were saying. Bease was holding Stargirl, and Claudia was petting the cat hesitantly.

At least Stargirl wasn't hissing or biting.

"He brought a stupid cat to impress a girl," said Jeremy. "What a Beasely!"

That's when Claudia kissed Bease—not on the forehead, or even the cheek, but right on the mouth.

"What?" said Jeremy. "She's just being nice."

"Claudia is nice," I agreed.

Claudia took the stinky cat from Bease's arms, and you would have thought she'd been given an academy award, she looked so happy. The two of them—no, three of them walked off as if they were in a world of their own.

"Uh," said Jeremy.

"What can I tell you, Jeremy," I replied. "Some guys got it."

Stargirl looked near dead the Sunday Bease found her, but it was eight years later when she finally passed peacefully away. I was there with Claudia and Tom (Claudia got everyone to stop calling him Bease), and their two children (who thankfully resembled their mother) as they laid her to rest in their back yard.

Bease was still girl-crazy, but his affection was limited to four girls now, Claudia, his little girls, Leia and Uhura, and Novagirl, a cat they kept from Stargirl's last litter.

Like her mother, Novagirl smelled bad and hissed whenever I came near. I didn't mind.

I'd learned never to criticize Bease's taste in girls.

Fluff vs. Scales

Courtney Annicchiarico

I was watching *Saved By The Bell* with Dad's pet snake, Charlie, wrapped around my wrist when Daddy came home with a little white box in his hand. As soon as I saw it, I jumped off the couch.

"Hi, Daddy."

"Hi, my girl." He jumped a little and tried to shift the box, still in his hand, casually behind him.

I tipped my chin in his direction and smiled. "What's in the box?"

His eyes cast around the room. "Just something for Charlie. Just some food."

"Ugh. Like bugs?" I shivered and crinkled my nose in distaste. I raised my wrist to the level of my face and spoke to Charlie. "You're lucky I love you."

Now that Mom and Dad had moved Charlie's tank to the living room, I guessed I'd have to deal with it.

"A snake has to eat, right?"

Charlie stretched his head forward and stuck out his tongue.

Daddy looked at the box in his hand and shook his head. "No, Charlie needs to eat something . . . else."

Fur, *Feathers,* and Scales

He pulled out a chair, sat down, and placed the box on the table. "I thought you knew. . . . Okay." Dad raked his hand through his hair. "Just peek in, okay?"

Now I saw that there were little holes in the sides of the box. I carefully lifted the cover and looked inside. Two little mice were huddled in a pile—white fluff and twitchy noses.

"Awww. They're so cute. But why did you—? Wait a minute. Are you going to feed *them* to Charlie?"

Daddy chewed on his lip for a moment, then nodded. "Sorry, baby."

I ran to Charlie's tank, pulled him from my wrist, and placed him on his rock. Returning to the table, I could barely control the quiver in my voice.

"Daddy, you can't. Please don't kill these mice. They're just babies. I'll take care of them, and Charlie will be fine. We'll just find something else for him to eat. Like crickets or spiders or something instead of . . ." I couldn't think of any other way to describe it. "Fluffy, little mice."

Mom came out of the kitchen and leaned against the wall.

"Mom, Dad wants to feed Charlie *mice.*"

"That won't really work, Brooker," Dad said. "I'm sorry. I thought you understood that boa constrictors eat mice. Plus . . . Charlie needs to hunt."

He got up, picked up the box, and moved toward the tank.

I jumped in front of him and held out my arms to block his way.

"You're just going to throw them in there? You're going to just let Charlie murder these innocent mice and . . . what . . . we're all going to just eat dinner in the other room like nothing absolutely . . . not . . . *humane* is happening?"

Dad glanced around for Mom, and I saw her mouth, "New spelling word."

"*This isn't funny.*" I burst into tears. "I can't believe this."

Fluff vs. Scales

Dad took a deep breath, let it out slowly, and knelt in front of me. "My girl, I don't love this part either, but this is what Charlie would eat if he were free."

"But I wouldn't have to *see* it."

"Sweetie," Mom said.

I didn't even notice that she had moved, but she was suddenly standing behind me with her arms around my shoulders.

"You don't have to watch. Do you want Dad to wait to put them in?"

"Or I could move Charlie's tank back to my room if that makes it easier," Dad added.

I shrugged away from her. "What good would that do? I'll still know what's going to happen."

Dad looked miserable, and I felt a little bad suddenly. So, I looked away and went back to Mom for that hug. I cried as quietly as I could, hiding my face against her shoulder, as I heard the tank lid open and, a moment later, snap back into place.

I went to bed without dinner. There was no way I could have eaten while I imagined how scared those little mice were. Were they trying to hide? Were they brothers and would one be sad when he saw the other eaten? If I had a brother, I would be sad. *It's no different,* I thought. I fell asleep thinking of the injustice and feeling brokenhearted that my dad was the cause.

The next morning, there was a little lump midway down Charlie and only one mouse left in the tank. My eyes locked on those little black eyes, and I resolved to find a way to save him. I had to play it cool and hide my intentions from my parents.

Fur, *Feathers,* and Scales

I didn't learn a thing in school. Instead of writing notes about Lewis and Clark or the proper use of modifiers, I brainstormed ideas in my notebook. Finally, during Algebra, inspiration struck. I scribbled frantically. I had the answer, and it was brilliant. Tons of people who used to eat meat do this, so why not a snake? Charlie would have to become a vegetarian.

Mom was waiting in the parking lot at three o'clock. *Keep it together. Just be casual.*

"Hi, Mom. Ummm . . . we're doing a kind of project in Health class. We have to keep a food journal of what we eat for five days, just a school week. So, I think we should have a lot of salad, veggies, and fruit to make it look good."

Mom brightened as she listened, like she was finally getting her life's biggest desire right there. "Sure thing. When is this supposed to start?"

"Well . . . tonight."

"Tonight? But it's Monday. We already did all the shopping for the week. Huh, you'd think Mr. Ellison would have given you guys some notice."

Oh, no. I could almost see Mom's thought bubble filling up as she composed a letter to my teacher on the spot. I pulled what I hoped was a sad look. "Well, he actually did, Mom. And I'm really sorry. I just completely forgot. And if I don't start turning stuff in, I'm going to get zeros."

That did it. Mom would never do anything to mess up my grades. "Ugh. I was going to just pick up Chinese tonight, because I was going to run over to Grandma's after dinner, but I guess we can do grilled chicken and a salad. Yeah, that's quick. Easy clean up. Okay."

It took a colossal effort to not sound disappointed. *Chinese? I love Chinese.* I blew out a breath and smiled. "Thanks, Mom."

We zipped through the supermarket, piling the cart with fresh and frozen veggies and fruit.

Fluff vs. Scales

When we got back to the house, I forced myself to ignore Charlie's tank. I helped Mom put the groceries away and chatted about my day, which was mostly just lies that spilled out because I had no idea what *really* happened. But the moment Mom went to the bathroom, I bolted to the tank. The little mouse was alert in the far corner, probably terrified. "Don't worry. I'm going to get you out of there. I promise. Just . . . try to stay away from Charlie." I looked at Dad's pet. He was sleeping.

During dinner, I kept an eye on the salad bowl and held my breath as Mom and Dad took seconds.

"Okay, Rich, I'll be ready to go to my mother's as soon as I clean up."

"I'll do it. You guys just go," I said as I stood up and started grabbing our plates off the table. "I'll do the dishes, too." Mom looked like she was going to faint, and Dad looked like he had just seen a unicorn on a unicycle. "It's just because you were so awesome about buying all this extra stuff and I feel bad about how I acted last night." I gave them my biggest smile. "So, don't get used to it."

Once they were out the door, I picked out a few lettuce leaves and some grated carrots. I approached the tank and dropped a leaf in front of Charlie. He wasn't interested at all. The little mouse was perched on top of Charlie's rock, not looking the least bit threatened. *Maybe Charlie's just not hungry,* I thought. I went back to the kitchen, grabbed a freezer bag, and filled it with as many dressing-free veggie pieces as I could salvage from the bowl and our dishes. I hid the bag in the back of the refrigerator and vowed to wake up early to feed Charlie again.

The next morning, I was showered and dressed before my parents' alarm went off. I was also discouraged. Again, Charlie refused to eat what I offered. Stupid snake.

I saved more veggies from my lunch and dinner, but my attempts to tempt Charlie that night and the following

Fur, *Feathers*, and Scales

morning were also failures. The mouse, at least, seemed calm. He obviously didn't see Charlie as a threat because he was curled up in a little white circle right out in the open. But, by the time I got home from school on Thursday, there was another little lump in Charlie.

Devastated, I decided that I would just have to free the next mouse and give Charlie no alternative to the vegetables I offered.

Brooding in my room, I figured out that Charlie must want to eat once about every four days, so I would just have to make sure I got any mice that Dad bought out of there before he got hungry.

At dinner, I casually asked Dad for what I hoped was a simple request. "Daddy, would you mind only putting one mouse in Charlie's tank at a time? I hated seeing that little mouse running around just waiting to be devoured."

"Sure, Brooker. You got it." I think he was so relieved just to do something for me that he would have done anything at that point.

I excused myself to finish up homework and tried not to think about all the mice that would die if I didn't make this work.

On Sunday, I took out my baggies of veggies and presented them to Charlie. I clapped my hand over my mouth to stifle my squeal. He ate some lettuce and little cubes of cucumber. That night, exactly as I had predicted, Dad brought home another mouse, but Charlie didn't seem to notice. I didn't dare risk leaving him in there, though. I went to my room to get a light jacket and asked Mom and Dad if I could walk down to the corner store to get an ice cream sandwich.

Dad left the room to get money, and Mom went into the kitchen to see if we needed more milk. As soon as I was alone, I scooped out the mouse and put it in my pocket. I lowered the lid shut just as Mom walked in to give me a

Fluff vs. Scales

short list of groceries to pick up. I took the money from Dad and went outside.

Relieved and finally able to exhale, as soon as I reached the grass on the side of the apartment building, I set the mouse free.

My plan was working. Every day, I left lettuce, cucumbers, and little bits of apple in Charlie's tank where Mom and Dad probably wouldn't notice but Charlie could find it.

By the time Dad put in the next mouse four days later, Charlie couldn't have cared less. I freed the mouse early in the morning, and Dad just assumed his snake had feasted during the night.

Charlie started hiding more and more, so maybe that's why Dad didn't notice that he was getting pretty thin. By the third week of my food swap and rescue, Charlie was just burying the food I'd leave, and I'd have to scoop it out whenever I had a free second. Then I started noticing some . . . well . . . liquidy poop. Probably just adjusting to the new diet, right?

But . . . what if he wasn't? I plucked Charlie off his rock and tried to urge him to wrap around my wrist, but he just stayed inactive in my hand. With a shock, I realized that I hadn't even played with Charlie even once since Dad came home with that first little, white box. "I'm so sorry for ignoring you, buddy."

I took him over to the couch, flipped on the TV, and settled down to watch whatever came on. I tried to coax Charlie into playing, but he only lay coiled in my lap. I missed my friend. Sure, he was technically Dad's snake, but he was mine, too. *What have I done?* I wondered as I stroked the top of his head. Finally, he stretched and slithered up to my shoulder and rested his head. I just prayed that meant we were friends again.

It was the day for Dad to put in a new mouse. I hated myself for doing it, but I left the mouse in there. Charlie hadn't eaten for days, and I had a sinking feeling that Charlie wasn't going to eat now either. By the second day, that little mouse was sleeping curled up next to Charlie and poor Charlie was barely moving.

"Dad?" I asked at dinner. "Do you think Charlie looks okay?"

Dad glanced at the tank. "I guess so. He seems to be pretty lethargic, but maybe he's getting ready to molt. He's eating okay. This mouse seems to be lucky, but the others were eaten within hours of me putting them in the tank. He just might not be hungry yet. Some snakes can go well over a week between feedings."

But I knew that wasn't it. I took a deep breath and told my parents everything about my plan to turn Charlie into a vegetarian.

"I thought he would get used to it. People do it all the time. But he hasn't eaten for a few weeks." Dad's eyes widened. Before he could say anything, I added, "I've been setting the mice free. I just couldn't stand to see those mice die."

"Courtney Brooke! Snakes are obligate carnivores. It means they can't even digest vegetables."

"How am I supposed to know that?" I started to cry, horrified. "Does that mean Charlie is really sick?"

"Yeah," Dad said, getting up from the table. "It may mean Charlie is dying."

Dying? My Charlie?

I spent the night in my room. Even if I hadn't been sent there, I couldn't bear to be around poor Charlie's empty tank. Dad had left to take Charlie to an animal hospital, and I held my breath every time I heard a car out on the street. Hours after I was supposed to be in bed, Dad finally came home. I ran out into the hallway and immediately started sobbing. Charlie's carrier was empty, and Dad was carrying a box.

Fluff vs. Scales

I flung myself into my dad's arms. "I killed him?"

Dad passed the box to Mom and hugged me tight. "No. No, you didn't. The vet gave him some medicine to help restore his digestion. He wants to keep Charlie there for a few days, but he's pretty sure Charlie will pull through."

I jumped up and down, laughter bursting out of me as my crying intensified. "When can we go get him?"

"Well, that depends. I called a few friends, and one of them agreed to adopt him if this is going to be too hard for you."

"No! I'll never take his mice away again! I love Charlie. And . . . I'll clean his tank, and play with him more, and . . ." I sobered and sheepishly smiled. "But maybe you could put Charlie's tank back in your room?"

Dad rolled his eyes but smiled. "You mean like I suggested weeks ago?" He hugged me and held me to him. "I can go one better. I'll get Charlie a second tank, one that is just for feeding, and I'll put that in my room. This way, you can still see Charlie most of the time, but you don't need to ever see the mice. And I have one more idea."

Dad took the box back from Mom, who was beaming, and gave it to me. I peered inside and sat down in the middle of the hallway. I scooped up the still-sleeping kitten and held her to my chest. "You got me a kitten?" I stared up at Dad. "I almost killed Charlie and you got me a kitten?"

Dad smiled and shrugged. "Yeah. Well . . . we're probably going to need some help keeping that colony of freed mice out of the building."

Why Children Have Their Father's Last Name

Marianne H. Donley

The Browns lived in a nice, soft rabbit hole, located in the very center of the dark green forest. Mr. and Mrs. Brown had two daughters who were as different as a silk purse and a sow's ear.

Charlotte was a very good little bunny. She did her best to make life pleasant. Charlotte always told the truth. Her manners were most correct. Charlotte was quiet, calm, and respectful.

Her sister, Sonja, was a very mischievous little bunny. She always did her best to make life exhilarating. Sonja thought that exaggerated stories were much more dramatic than the "real" truth. Her manners were most casual. Sonja was exciting, boisterous, and unconventional.

The Brown sisters grew up and married.

Charlotte, the good little bunny, married Reggie, a very mischievous little rabbit. He did his best to make life exhilarating. Reggie thought that exaggerated stories were much more dramatic than the "real" truth. His manners were most casual. He was exciting, boisterous, and unconventional.

Fur, *Feathers*, and Scales

Sonja, the mischievous little bunny, married Julius, a good little rabbit. He did his best to make life pleasant. Julius always told the truth. His manners were most correct. Julius was quiet, calm, and respectful.

Soon Mr. and Mrs. Brown had six little grandchildren hopping around their nice, soft rabbit hole, located in the very center of the dark green forest.

Charlotte and Reggie had three very mischievous little rabbits. Three little rabbits who did their best to make life exhilarating. They all thought that exaggerated stories were much more dramatic than the "real" truth. Their manners were most casual. Those three little rabbits were exciting, boisterous, and unconventional.

Sonja and Julius had three good little bunnies. Three little bunnies who did their best to make life pleasant. They always told the truth. Their manners were most correct. Those thee little bunnies were quiet, calm, and respectful.

Moral: You always get the children your husband deserves.

Unnatural

Carol L. Wright

I was ill-prepared for what happened. I see now that it was all my fault. I fell prey to my own delusions, one being that within this town I could find a place of my own, beyond the prying eyes of my neighbors and the judgment of the church.

I should have known better. I have no excuse. I was no longer young. At thirty-two, and the mother of four, I should have taken my responsibilities more seriously and not permitted myself to stray so far beyond the strictures of our church.

I say "our" church, even though I was never deemed worthy of membership. My husband, Robert, is a member, but the Reverend Hooker holds things in my past against me, for which no fault was truly mine.

I was seeking to be a good member of my former community when I warned that my neighbor, Goodwife Bailey, was consorting with Satan. But it was we who had to leave that place in disgrace and settle in Farmington to start anew. Imagine that horrid woman accusing *me* of the capital offense of adultery simply to bring shame upon our house. Although no action was taken against me, I wish I could have received an acquittal of those charges to clear my name. I wonder whether that would have softened Reverend Hooker's heart towards me and spared me my fate.

But how glad I was when we first came to this place. The forests surrounding the town were lush and fragrant in the spring, alive with all of Creation. Birdsong filled my heart with gladness. Could it really be so sinful to burst forth in dance when it is inspired by God's creatures? Of course, I was always careful to keep these expressions of joy concealed from my neighbors—or so I thought. If only I had known Goody Greensmith had espied me.

Whenever chance permitted, I would steal away from my labors, caring for the mistress's baby while my eldest watched her siblings at home. Even though I knew it was a sin to lie to the mistress, I would create some excuse to escape to the forest when the babe napped. And, often, I would stop there on my way to or from our small, unpainted house on the edge of the wood at the beginning and end of each day.

It was when I was there in the woods that I learned a secret that few humans have been privy to. A doe trusted me so well as to allow me near her fawn. His spotted coat made him almost invisible in the dappled sunlight, yet suddenly, there he was. His steady gaze showed no fear, and I felt a thrill of acceptance I had never known in our human community.

People might think it unnatural for such a relationship to occur, but isn't it the way nature should always be? Don't the scriptures say that the wolf shall dwell with the lamb? I am sure I have heard that during the long church services I am obligated to attend, even if I cannot be a member.

The dark eyes of the fawn inspected me, embraced me. His spirit was strong, and I knew he would grow to lead a mighty herd, evading the guns of the townsfolk during their hunting forays. Somehow, I knew. So did the doe. We shared a pride in her offspring. I grew to love the fawn almost as much as my own youngest, Hannah. Certainly, more than the mistress's baby, who was more toil than pleasure. The more I saw of the fawn, the more I had to see him. Our souls connected—even if the Reverend Hooker has proclaimed that animals have no souls.

Humans are not all vile sinners as the Reverend Hooker preaches. We are made in the image of God. Why, therefore, are there such strict rules of behavior that seem designed to separate us from the beauty of Creation? How can our natural inclinations also be "depraved," as the Reverend says?

These are blasphemous thoughts, I know. They rose unbidden to my ignorant mind. Perhaps if I were wiser, I could understand. Perhaps if I were more pious, I could fight the impulses that draw me back to nature. Perhaps if I were purer, these thoughts would never form.

I am flawed; that I own. But is it too sinful of me to believe that the Reverend Hooker be also flawed?

Perhaps I did tarry too long in the woods. The mistress's babe did not sleep so long during the day as my children had at that age. If she awoke before my return, the mistress would be in high dudgeon. She harbored an unnatural meanness in her. Most often her wrath would fall upon me, but when I wasn't there, I feared the babe bore the brunt of it.

When I returned after too long a time away, she screamed at me that the babe was ill. I went to the child and found her not fully awake and her complexion blue. She had trouble drawing breath and when she could, she spent it fussing. I tried my best for her, but God called her home. Mistress went into a fury, raging and striking me for killing her child. It could have been her grief, not her meanness, that caused her to speak thus.

I knew my presence brought her no solace, so I left for home. She followed me, hurling curses at me that I would not want my children to hear, so I diverted my path toward the wood, believing she would not follow me there. I was right; she turned toward town.

Once in the wood, I knelt by a rock and cried for the lost child. The small buck appeared and comforted me. Such a good soul has he.

I tarried long there, seeking comfort from nature and from God. When Reverend Hooker and the constable came for me, grabbed me, and tore me away from my beloved fawn, the deer stood his ground, stomping his hoof and snorting in a manner beyond his age. If the situation were less serious, I would have laughed to see he, who yet had no antlers and whose baby spots were still fading, endeavor to appear so fierce.

"Witch," they cried. "Thou shouldst die for thine evil deeds."

I knew not what to say, so remained silent, giving a last, longing look at the fawn as they forced me out of the woods and into the prison where others so accused languished awaiting trial.

Within a week, my trial took place in the log building in the center of town—the Meeting House. Stocks and a whipping post at the front of the building awaited those accused of lesser offenses.

My trial began with a reading of the accusation. "Thou art here indicted by the name of Mary Barnes for not having the fear of God before thine eyes, thou hast entertained familiarity with Satan, the grand enemy of God and mankind—and by his help has acted things in a preternatural way beyond human abilities in a natural course for which according to the law of God and the established law of this commonwealth thou deservest to die."

My nerves were so disturbed, I knew not what to do. I heard them say that two witnesses were required to put me to death. I believed they had only the mistress's word, which gave me comfort. Then I heard that another in the

Unnatural

prison, Mrs. Greensmith, had also accused me. She was a confessed witch and condemned to death before my trial. Why, therefore, would they accept her word?

She said that she had seen me dance in the woods in the company of a familiar—a creature given to me by the Devil to help me execute my evil deeds. Whatever could she have meant? I admit that I had danced, but only when alone. I had heard that a crow could be such a creature, but I remembered no crows in the forest.

"And what shape did this familiar take," the questioner inquired.

She looked at me with an evil glint in her eye as she answered. "The shape of a fawn. A baby deer."

I know my face turned pale, for I felt likely to faint. How could she ascribe any evil to my beloved deer?

Mrs. Greensmith was not done with her condemnation. "It calls her into the woods, and she obeys its commands. It invites her to dance for it, and she dances with abandon. She expresses an unnatural love for it, stroking its fur and embracing it in a depraved manner that could only come from the Devil."

I knew then that Goodwife Greensmith told the truth. I was guilty. I had not known myself to be a witch. I had believed myself to be doing the work of God—not of the Devil.

Then I heard the charge to the jury. "According to the Code of Law of 1650 governing the colony of Connecticut, 'If any man or woman be a witch, that is have consultation with a familiar spirit, they shall be put to death.'"

And so, it was decided.

This morning, Goodwife Greensmith, her husband, and I were loaded onto an ox cart and taken to gallows hill. The townsfolk gathered there pelted us with rotted fruit and chanted, "Witch, witch, witch." Many times, I heard our souls consigned to Hell.

Fur, *Feathers*, and Scales

I looked for my children in the crowd but was relieved when I did not see them. They need not see their mother die in this manner. My dear Robert also was not there. I would not wish to add to his grief, but it would have brought me some succor to have seen his smile one more time.

I scaled the scaffold behind the Greensmiths. A noose was placed on Goody Greensmith's neck. She glared at me as she was pushed off the platform. She struggled, kicking her feet and swinging in a wide arc. After some moments, she was still. Mr. Greensmith was next. He looked down and once the noose was secured, leaped to his fate with vigor, not waiting to be pushed. He swung on his rope but did not struggle. Then it was my turn.

I feared that my legs would give way as they pushed me closer to the rope. I turned my face towards the forest in the distance. What was it I saw there as the noose closed around my neck? The fawn. I could feel his eyes upon me.

I knew he was of the Devil, but I could not but smile.

Tipping Point

A. E. Decker

Forget the slinky, red, off-the-shoulder dress. The only article of Sherilynn Cabot's clothing I wanted to see her remove was her shoes.

Yes, but how to arrange that small miracle? I asked myself as I arranged peapod-wrapped shrimp on a small plate. She clearly adored the damn, tippy, spike-heeled things; took every opportunity to hook them over my sofa's arms and admire them under the studio lights. Probably, part of the attraction for her was knowing her ex was under scrutiny at work for lifting them.

Sighing, I picked up the plate.

I smelled burning.

The lasagna! But, when my gaze snapped toward the oven, no tendrils of smoke curled out its door. The cause of the charred smell was something far worse.

I wasted two seconds staring at the scorched item lying on the counter before bolting for the living room. I lost momentum when I stubbed my prosthetic—not one I wore often—against a chair leg. I reached the doorway in time to see Sherilynn tip the last of her Riesling into Zeppelin's aquarium.

She was trying to murder my cuttlefish!

Fur, *Feathers,* and Scales

I didn't strangle her on the spot. *I won't strangle her on the spot*, I insisted, sucking air through my nose. My guts cramped like I'd gulped icy water from Zep's tank. The peapod-wrapped shrimp rattled softly on the plate.

That small noise must've alerted Sherilynn to my presence. She whirled, hand flying to her lips. For a long second, we locked gazes. Then, her eyes narrowed in calculation.

She giggled, and I knew—knew like I could tell a nautilus from an argonaut at a glance—what tactic she'd try. "Ooh, Caleb, I already finished my delicious Pinot Noir," she said, holding up her glass. "Fetch me another?"

Gaslighting—right on target. Am I good, or what? "Sure," I said, plastering a smile over my teeth. "But let's get you back to the sofa first." I offered my arm.

"Such a gentlemen," she cooed, accepting it.

"You're welco—"

"Especially since I can walk better than you can," she added with a naughty giggle and a shampoo commercial-worthy toss of her blonde locks.

If I was less of a professional, I'd have demonstrated how deft I was with my prosthetic by using it to boot her the rest of the way to the sofa. But I am a professional, and Sherilynn—unbeknownst to her—was my latest client.

"Undoubtedly," I gritted out sweetly, navigating her successfully around my glass coffee table. Once she was safely seated on my squashy blue sofa, I set the peapod shrimp before her. Sherilynn grabbed three before I could say "Help yourself." Hooking her ankles over the sofa's arm, she admired her black-and-silver Jimmy Choos.

Stiletto heels. Pointy toes. Thin, slippery soles. Hands down the *worst* possible footwear for traversing slick gray tile, which, coincidentally, was exactly the surface covering my living room floor. I know most people chose carpeting, but most people don't own an eighteen-inch cuttlefish with a habit of squirting water everywhere when he gets in a

Tipping Point

snit. It was because of those shoes, and not any misguided notions of chivalry, that I'd escorted her to the sofa. I didn't want her to break her neck before I had a chance to save it, so to speak.

Of course, if she didn't leave Zep alone, I'd find myself strongly tempted to break it myself.

The memory of her pouring wine into his tank made my jaw clench anew. "I'll fetch you a fresh glass," I told her, rubbing my neck. "You just stay there—right there—and relax."

Giving no sign she'd heard me, she took out a compact and studied her own prettiness.

At least it's a sedentary occupation, I thought, picking up her glass.

On my way to the kitchen, I paused by Zep's aquarium. He hung six inches above its sandy bottom, his eight arms hanging relaxed, fins undulating gently. Cephalopods are sensitive creatures. The slightest change in copper levels in the water is generally cause for panic.

Zeppelin, however, is immortal, so a single glass of Riesling—*not* Pinot Noir, by the way—filtered through his two-hundred-and-fifty-gallon tank wouldn't harm him the slightest. The real fear was that he'd decide he liked it, subjecting me to the tantrums of an aquatic lush.

When I raised two fingers in the "victory" salute, Zep casually mimicked the gesture with two arms.

He's okay. Relieved, I continued into the kitchen, where the lasagna's savory smell mingled with my apartment's omnipresent briny odor—courtesy of Zep—and the continuing, acrid scent of smoke from the ledger still smoldering on the counter.

I didn't need to stagger over to it, but it felt appropriate. Once there, I simply fell forward, catching myself against the counter's edge. I took a fortifying breath before reading the new tally scrawled across the bottom of the yellowing paper.

It was on the largish side, and pulsed bright red.

Shit.

None of the religions have gotten it exactly right, but there *is* an afterlife, consisting of the Place You Want to Go ... and the Other Place. I know this because I work for the guy who runs the Other Place.

I don't trick people into selling their souls, or anything miserable like that. Seriously, why would I bother? Take a look at the people running our country lately, for instance. My boss is positively drowning in tarnished souls. He's just tired of getting all the schmucks.

So, a century or two ago, he started hiring people to approach the borderline cases and improve their tallies enough for them to get into the Place You Want to Go. Let The Big Guy Upstairs handle a few of the petty thieves, shallow narcissists, and blowhard reality TV stars with bad comb-overs, he figured. (Both sides really hate comb-overs. I believe you earn a percentage of Bad Points for every day you scrape your last three hairs over the spotlight on your head.)

Far from mining for souls, I'm actually doing Good ... even if I'm working for the Big Bad. And while I'm still debating the ethics myself, one of the consequences of my job is that when my clients die, their final tally gets added to mine.

Sherilynn's new, red number pulsed sardonically between my palms.

Growling, I pushed off the counter and went to chop vegetables for the salad. *I need time to figure out how to fix this mess,* I thought, attacking the carrots. Time that, by definition, I didn't have. I don't *get* clients until they're nearing their end and the question of exactly where they're headed once the bell rings becomes an issue. Usually, I

Tipping Point

figure I have thirteen days to tip my client's tally upward. The boss likes the number thirteen. In Sherilynn's case—

Blowing out my cheeks, I set the knife down and ran a hand through my hair. Yeah. In Sherilynn's case, I received her file from my case manager, Big Paul, the very same day that my friend Danika in Puget Sound set up an underwater camera trained on a nesting giant Pacific octopus. Naturally, I'd only taken a brief glance at Sherilynn's file and marked it down as an easy case before tossing it aside and spending the next nine days camped before my laptop, watching Mama Octopus tend her eggs. Who could resist an opportunity like that?

All right, I suppose a lot of people could. I don't pretend to understand them. Within those nine days, Sherilynn committed adultery with a drinking buddy, cajoled her ex into shoplifting those Jimmy Choos, and swiped a cookie from an annoying child and fed it to a dog—which didn't count against her too badly, because the child *was* annoying, and at least she was nice to the dog. Let me tell you, when I finally surfaced from octo-watching and noticed the change in her tally, I dropped my cup of coffee right into my lap.

Picking up the knife, I resumed chopping more slowly. I'd never failed the boss before. Sherilynn may not have been a smuggler or a pop idol, but Big Paul had hinted the boss really didn't want her hanging around his place. What would he do if he learned she'd only traveled downward because I'd blown off her case to watch an octopus? I wasn't sure the boss fully appreciated cephalopods, although he had made Zep immortal as a bonus after I'd redirected a really tacky game show host with a terrible combover in only three days.

A trickle of smoke wafted over the chopping board. I waved it away, not needing the reminder that Sherilynn's attempted poisoning of Zep was the crowning jellyfish in her demerit punchbowl. The Good and Bad Sides can quibble over theft and adultery, but both agree that trying to murder a person's pet is just plain *low*.

But a second puff of smoke ambled after the first. *Oh, crap, did she commit some other vile deed while I dithered here?* My head snapped toward her ledger.

Its edge was brown and crumbly.

I froze, the knife quivering in my hand. A sliver of radish clung to a knuckle. Clients' files turn to ash when they die. This preliminary singeing indicated Sherilynn had hours left. At best. *Those damn shoes.* Or—

What the hell had I been thinking, giving her shrimp for an appetizer? People choked on shrimp all the time. She could be out there now, clutching her throat.

(Actually, I'd gotten the shrimp for Zep, but he'd refused them, knowing I had crabs in the holding tank. If Sherilynn choked to death, it served me right for being cheap.)

Tearing a scrap off Sherilynn's file, I stuffed it in my sleeve and sprinted back to the living room, mentally reviewing the Heimlich maneuver. But instead of sprawled over my sofa, gone blue as its cushions, Sherilynn again stood precariously before Zep's aquarium, fists knuckled on her hips.

At least she isn't peeing into the water or something, I thought, approaching her softly so as not to spook her into jumping. "Sorry for taking so long," I said.

She turned, a scowl torquing her painted lips. "What kind of fish did you say this was?"

"A common cuttlefish," I replied. *Sepia officinalis.* Zep hovered by his corals, fins barely moving. Cuttlefish resemble an octopus stuffed inside a football with frills sewn down both sides. His skin shimmered, smooth and mottled silver, brown, and gray.

Maybe this was my way in. If Zep intrigued her, I could cultivate an interest in some environmental cause. A char-

Tipping Point

itable donation to whale rescue or turtle sanctuaries would quickly earn her a heap of Good Points.

"He's not a fish at all, actually," I began. "Cuttlefish are cephalopods—"

"It's weird," she sniffed, and stomped back to the sofa.

So much for that. I tried to exchange a disgruntled look with Zep, but he turned a cranky shade of brown and picked at a pebble. On the positive side, Sherilynn made it back to the sofa without slipping. Sprawling across all three cushions, she pouted, twirling a lock of hair around a finger.

I took the armchair next to her. I'd forgotten her wine, but I didn't dare leave her alone again. She was likely regretting accepting the dinner invite from the crippled fish nerd. If I wasn't—all modesty aside—a good-looking cripple, dark-haired, with startlingly pale blue eyes and dusky skin, she probably never would have agreed. I had little doubt that as soon as she'd scarfed the greater share of the lasagna, she'd remember she'd forgotten to vacuum her cat or something and bolt.

And get hit by a bus, leaving me to explain to the boss how she ended up in his place, I thought.

No way. There had to be a scrap of goodness hidden inside her. I just had to coax it into the sunlight. "Tell me about yourself," I said, moving the plate of shrimp out of her reach. Only one remained, but there's no harm in caution.

Lighting up like I'd hit her "on" switch, Sherilynn began to speak.

Five minutes later, I was revisiting the murder option I'd briefly considered earlier. *No wonder the boss doesn't want her in his place,* I thought, listening to her story, liberally sprinkled with naughty-girl giggles, about how she'd once mixed pigeon dung into Madelaine-something-or-other's foundation cream, just because Madelaine took her favorite parking spot.

Fur, *Feathers,* and Scales

"Wow, poor Madelaine," I attempted. "She must've—"
"And then Jaqueline and Jim started fighting. Ooh!" Sherilynn giggled. "I saw my chance."
"Surely Madelaine—"
"Jim always had a thing for me." Giggling, Sherilynn wound her hair around her finger and surged ahead.
Can *ears* glaze over? I think mine did. I was beginning to believe an earthquake could swallow Baltimore, and as the buildings collapsed around us, Sherilynn would keep talking (and talking and *talking!*) and the last thing I'd hear would be that giggle.
"Bloomingdales had to take the dress back, of course," Sherilynn chattered on. "They never noticed the stain, and I used the refund to buy—"
I squeezed my eyes shut. *Come on, earthquake. Do it, do it.* Surely, I'd earned enough Good Points from my other jobs that Sherilynn and I would go to the opposite Places after Baltimore sank into the sea. I'd take comfort in the fact that it was her attempted assassination of Zep that ultimately tipped her into perdition.
"So, I said to Bernice—" Sherilynn broke off with a gasp.
My eyes flew open. "What?" I asked, professional pride reasserting itself in a flash. I feared she'd suffered some seizure and was about to collapse in front of me.
She pointed a shaking finger at Zep's tank. "It turned into a demon!"
I looked. Zep floated in the exact same position before his corals, staring out at the room with apparent disinterest.
Pushing off the sofa, Sherilynn jogged to the tank. I jumped up also, meaning to catch her if she slipped.
My quick motion twisted my prosthetic slightly askew. Normally, I'd have sat and readjusted it, but I couldn't do that with Sherilynn galumphing over my tiled floor. Gritting my teeth, I limped to her side. "Demon?" I said.

Tipping Point

Inside the tank, Zep hovered, his W-shaped pupils fixed on some point past Sherilynn's shoulder. No one can ignore you like a cuttlefish. They can muster an indifference so deep, almost primeval, that you might doubt your own existence. Zep usually only blanked me when I did something completely offensive, like offer him a piece of frozen shrimp.

"It was red and spikey," Sherilynn insisted, clearly thinking I doubted her.

I didn't. Cuttlefish are masters of camouflage. Chameleons? Amateurs. In addition to changing their color, cuttlefish can shift their skin's texture by raising little bumps called papillae. I believed she'd seen exactly what she claimed; I just wondered why Zep had put on the display.

But I could work with demon. Ignoring the increasingly strident pain in my left leg, I rubbed my chin. "Demon, huh?" I said, putting on a worried look. If you can convince a person they're seeing demons, you can get them worrying about the things they've done to attract said demons. From there, it's a straight path to convincing them to mend their ways. Although it gets tricky here—deeds done out of self-interest don't merit Good Points. If they did, I could just hand my clients their files, tell them to buy candy for orphan children, and watch Mama Octopus in peace.

I could have saved my acting skills. All Sherilynn's attention focused on Zep, who continued hanging at the front of his tank, motionless save for the undulation of his fins. His complete dismissal of our presence rolled over us in near-tangible waves. "Primates?" he seemed to be saying. "Ha! An amusing fairy tale, but it doesn't fool me."

"What's it doing?" Sherilynn demanded.

I didn't bother replying, partially because I'd learned better than to try it by now, but mostly because I was wondering myself. Usually, when I have company, Zep begs for food by wiggling his mantle, starfishing his arms, and kissing the glass. Then, after he's gotten his treat and my guest comes over for a better look at him, he dashes behind his corals and hides.

Why aren't you following your usual routine? I bent closer, squinting at him. Had the wine affected him after all?

Or—

Three small papillae spiked above Zep's eye on his left side. Sherilynn couldn't possibly see them from the angle she stood at. They vanished as quickly as they formed, and Zep resumed his posture of utter indifference.

Had he just winked at me?

Zep's almost four years old. In cuttlefish terms, that translates to "should've been dead three years ago." Could Zep somehow have realized he'd outlived his due date? Recent research indicates cuttlefish can count up to five, so maybe Zep had been ticking off days inside his odd, doughnut-shaped brain. We really don't know how smart cephalopods are. Perhaps they've been laughing at our antics all along. And if they're *that* smart, and Zep had been granted all that extra time to hone his intellect . . .

I often took my clients' files into the living room and read them aloud. Just possibly, Zep had been listening.

I peeked at the scrap of Sherilynn's file tucked in my sleeve. A bit of its edge crumbled off, clinging to my wrist. What the heck. None of my attempts had paid off. Let Zep take his shot.

Still scowling, Sherilynn waved at Zep. He didn't react. Non-existent primates couldn't wave, after all. Next, she smacked the glass. I winced, fearing Zep would rocket backward and injure himself against the corals. That's what a normal cuttlefish would do. But Zep's fins kept rippling smoothly. Whatever he was contemplating existed in a world far beyond this one, with its silly, imaginary primates.

Tipping Point

Sherilynn's brows drew down. Her lips pushed out. Before this, she probably couldn't have conceived of a universe she wasn't the center of, let alone one where she didn't exist. Being ignored, thoroughly and completely ignored—even by a strange, wiggly-legged, blimp-shaped fish—was more than she could bear.

"I hate that thing!" she burst out and started to flounce away.

The instant she turned, Zep flamed orange-red. Spikey papillae popped up all over his body while larger, horn-like ones sprouted above his eyes. Stretching out all his arms, he waggled them like a fistful of snakes.

Sherilynn shrieked. I couldn't entirely blame her. Zep had managed to transform himself into something you'd expect to see in the skankier corners of the Other Place. But even as she spun back to face him, his skin smoothed out, fading to mottled silver-gray-brown.

Face contorted, Sherilynn reached down to yank off one of her shoes.

"Hey!" I cried as she raised it. I caught her wrist just before she brought that pointy heel crashing down into the aquarium's glass side.

We grappled on the smooth tiles. She wore only one high-heeled shoe. The stump of my left leg grated in my prosthetic's socket.

It was inevitable that we slipped.

I didn't waste time cursing when I felt our balance shift; just grabbed her head, cradled it to my chest, and curled my spine to absorb the shock of landing best as possible. My upper back struck the solid wooden base supporting Zep's aquarium, but at least I didn't crack my skull against the glass.

Sherilynn lay utterly still in my grip a moment, knocked briefly breathless, I think, by the impact. She must've hit her knees pretty hard. The next instant she was pushing away, beating at me with her fists. "Let go of me, you—ooh!" Her eyes rounded. She put a knuckle to her mouth. "Ooh, that's . . . ooh!"

These "oohs" didn't have the syrupy, manipulative tone of her earlier ones. I followed her gaze to my left leg. Our fall had knocked my prosthetic to a disturbing, completely wrong-looking angle.

"Are you . . . is that . . ." Sherilynn floundered.

I was *fine*. It wasn't a problem. I could've sat there and readjusted my prosthetic, or scooted across the floor to a chair, as I'd done a hundred times over.

I'm perfectly abled. It battered around inside my mouth like an angry butterfly, but I bit it back, because something that resembled sympathy had blossomed in Sherilynn's face. The scrap of paper pressed against my wrist cooled just a trifle.

I don't need help. Taking a breath, I swallowed the words. "Could you help me to the chair, please?"

Sherilynn hesitated. Then, without speaking, she removed her remaining Jimmy Choo and set it with the one that had fallen beside the coffee table. Putting an arm around my waist, she helped me rise and hobble to the chair.

The scrap of paper hidden in my sleeve cooled noticeably.

"Thank you," I said, dropping into the chair. I glanced at the tank. Zep bobbed slowly up and down, a few blue streaks appearing amongst his brown-and-gray stripes.

Perched on the sofa's edge, hands tucked between her knees, Sherilynn watched me unstrap my prosthetic. "Does it hurt?"

My stump throbbed a little, from the pinching and the fall, but I shook my head. "No. Does it disturb you?"

Tipping Point

She nibbled her lower lip. "No." I pulled off my stump sleeve and she grimaced and averted her gaze from the folded, pink scar. "Well, it's kind of gross."

My teeth started to clamp down. I forced my jaw to relax and laughed instead. "Yeah, it is. But still, I'm lucky." Leaning over, I checked my limb for any sign of swelling. "I was in a bus crash." (I was hit by a motorcycle.) "Robbie, this little boy sitting near me, lost both his legs." (The guy who hit me was drunk, but then, so was I.)

No response from Sherilynn. Crap, had she gotten bored? Was she admiring herself in her compact again? I looked up. Sherilynn's mouth and eyes were round.

"*Both* of them?" she asked.

Holy cephalopods; she'd actually listened. "Both," I said. Then, since the story was already pretty rich, I decided I might as well toss a few more eggs in the batter. "Above the knees, too, poor kid," I added, heaving a sigh as I pulled my sock back on. "His family didn't have good insurance, either. Thank goodness there are charities that help pay for 3D printed prosthetics these days. Even so—"

"I've heard of those!" Sherilynn whipped out her smartphone. Holding my breath, I worked on my prosthetic, expecting her to get distracted by an ad for expensive face cream or something. But a moment later, she flipped her phone around. "Is that the one?"

I peered at the screen. "I think so. I'll ask Robbie the next time I e-mail him."

Turning the phone back to herself, she tapped it a few times. The scrap against my wrist cooled. I quietly released my breath even before she lifted her head, smiling in triumph. "You can tell him I made a donation, too."

"Thank you," I said. Said it from the heart, too, and maybe she sensed it, because her smile widened. "Robbie will be so grateful." (If he existed, that is.) Securing my prosthetic's last strap, I stood. "The lasagna should be ready. I'll check."

Still smiling, Sherilynn reached down and retrieved her shoes.

What I really wanted to check was her ledger. Had her act of charity been enough to tip her balance? It couldn't be by much, if it was. And if it was enough, how did I prevent her from reverting to form and dumping salt in my wine, or some other act of petty spite before her time ran out?

Preoccupied, I paused on my way to the kitchen to lightly rap my knuckles against Zep's tank. "Nice going, buddy," I whispered. If he hadn't schooled Sherilynn on the horrors of being ignored, she might never have listened to my fabricated tale.

Rising to the tank's top, Zep aimed his siphon and directed a stream of water over the edge.

"*Ooh!*" cried Sherilynn.

I knew immediately this particular "ooh" was different from the rest. It was shrill and terrified and ended abruptly in a tinkling crash. I whirled around. Sherilynn lay sprawled in a ruin of glass from my coffee table. I stared at the small puddle collected on the tiles, at the moisture staining the soles of her Jimmy Choos, before racing into the kitchen to grab her ledger.

It crumbled in my hands, but not before I'd seen the final tally. Picking up my phone, I dialed 9-1-1. It didn't take long to give them the address.

Then, I returned to the living room and faced Zep, drifting in his tank. "How did you know?" I asked. Those scientists needed to redo their research, because I had reason to suspect cuttlefish were more talented with numbers than merely counting to five.

Three-tenths of a Good Point. That's all that tipped Sherilynn's balance in the end. As far as my own tally was concerned, it probably wouldn't make any difference in the

Tipping Point

world. But who knows? It had made all the difference in the afterworld to Sherilynn.

Picking up the last peapod-wrapped shrimp, I raised it to her in salute. "Enjoy your eternal reward," I said. Perhaps she was already telling the angels about the time she mixed canola oil into Sally-whatsit's shampoo.

I peeled off the peapod and popped it in my mouth. Reaching into the tank, I offered Zep the shrimp. He flared red. Papillae spiked all over his body. Then, all at once, he smoothed out. His mottling returned. Spreading two arms in a cephalopod shrug, he extended his tentacles and nabbed the shrimp. I leaned back against his tank. Munching in companionable silence, we waited for the ambulance to arrive.

If I get a bonus for this job, I'm asking for an eternal octopus.

Doeg's Story

Will Wright

Outside an upper window of a great mansion, a fat, gray bird sat awaiting the morning sun. On his leg was a thin, golden tether that led into the mansion through a window.

A scarlet songbird landed farther along the branch from the gray. It looked like a fine place to spend a moment. Below the tree was an immaculate garden lined with small, silver markers. The pretty markers glowed faintly in the predawn.

The songbird opened her mouth and sang a song of first light. Though she was tiny, her voice filled the garden. She sang of the deep blue that covered the sky, how it quivered and waited for the first hint of light. She sang of bold beams bursting from the east and racing across the horizon, waking bird and beast. Finally, she sang of the infant sun raising its head, looking with newness and wonder at the earth before it.

"That was lovely," said the gray bird. "Will you teach it to me?"

"Why do you want to learn my song?" asked the songbird. "Don't you have a morning song of your own?"

"I have many songs," said the gray bird. "I am a collector bird. My master feeds me well and dotes on me because

I have learned songs and stories from many birds. My master will love me better if I learn your song of first light."

"But I am hungry," said the scarlet bird. "I have sung the song of first light, and now I must find seed to eat."

"I have lovely seed within this window," said the gray bird. "My master gives me all the seed that I desire. If you will teach me your song of first light, I will bring you seed such as you have never tasted before."

"I do not trust that window," said the songbird. "Though I don't wish to judge you, I don't know if it's good that any bird have a master. Still, if you wish to learn the song, I will teach you, for the song is beautiful and should be sung."

"I will bring out the seed," said the gray.

The two birds ate, and true to the collector bird's promise, it was a most excellent selection of seeds. Though the scarlet bird was sleepy from the feast, she kept her bargain and taught the gray bird the song of first light.

Though the collector bird was plain, he had a magnificent range and learned to sing the song very quickly.

"You have learned very well," said the scarlet bird.

"Thank you," said the gray. "Do you know any other songs?"

It was just past noon, and the scarlet songbird opened her mouth and sang the song of midday. Though she was tiny, her voice carried over the midday bustle. She sang of the wide vistas she could see from her branch. She sang of clouds rolling on their journeys of changing and becoming. She sang of birds and beasts busy with the toils of life, some with little ones in tow. She sang of the sun in its prime ripening the grain, drying the dew, and brightening every corner of the earth.

"That was lovely," said the gray bird. "Will you teach it to me?"

"Why do you want to learn my song?" asked the songbird. "Don't you have a midday song of your own?"

Doeg's Story

"I have many songs," said the gray bird. "I am a collector bird. My master feeds me well and dotes on me because I have learned songs and stories from many birds. My master will love me better if I learn your song of midday."

"But I must build a nest," said the scarlet bird. "If I am to have young, I must gather twigs and grasses and leaves to weave."

"I have lovely strands within this window," said the gray bird. "My master gives me all the cotton, wool, linen, and silk that I could desire. You see how lovely this tether is that I wear. If you will teach me your song of midday, I will bring you strands of unsurpassed beauty and comfort for your nest."

"I still do not trust your window," said the songbird. "Your tether is beautiful, but it fills me with dread. Still, if you wish to learn the song, I will teach you, for the song is beautiful and should be sung."

"I will bring out the strands," said the gray.

The two birds wove, and it was a most excellent selection of fibers. Together they built a magnificent nest. Though the scarlet bird longed to find a mate to bring to her nest, she kept her bargain and taught the gray bird the song of midday.

Though the collector bird was plain, he had a magnificent range and learned to sing the song very quickly.

"You have learned very well," said the scarlet bird.

"Thank you," said the gray. "Do you know any other songs?"

It was evening now, and the sun was about to set. The scarlet songbird opened her mouth and sang the song of day's end. Though she was tiny, her voice carried into the mansion. She sang of long shadows reaching from tree to tree. She sang of flowers closing, birds nesting, and beasts burrowing. She sang of human lights, invisible in the full day, dotting the land like raspberries on a bush. She sang of the ancient sun, tired from its labors, resting in a bed of many colors.

"That was lovely," said the gray bird. "Will you teach it to me?"

"Why do you want to learn my song?" asked the songbird. "Don't you have an evening song of your own?"

"I have many songs," said the gray bird. "I am a collector bird. My master feeds me well and dotes on me because I have learned songs and stories from many birds. My master will love me better if I learn your song of day's end."

"But I must sleep," said the scarlet bird. "If I am to rise and sing the song of first light, my eyes must be bright, and my heart rested."

"Within this window," said the gray bird, "my master has taught me a great secret of rest. It is a rest so complete that you need not fear weariness in the morning. If you teach me your song of day's end, I will teach you this secret, and you will rest so fully that you will not miss the sleep you lost."

"I do not trust your window," said the songbird. "A peaceful rest is a joy, but my rest is usually sweet; I do not need this secret. Still, if you wish to learn, I will teach you, for the song is beautiful and should be sung."

"Teach me, then," said the gray, "and the secret will be yours."

This time the gray would not tell his secret until he learned the song. Even so, the scarlet bird held back her slumber and kept the bargain. She taught the gray bird the song of day's end.

Though the collector bird was plain, he had a magnificent range and learned to sing the song very quickly.

"You have learned very well," said the scarlet bird.

"Thank you," said the gray. "Do you know any other songs?"

Doeg's Story

"I know no other songs," said the scarlet bird. "I only wish you peace with what you've learned. You may keep your secret of rest. I will fly now and find my rest."

"But your nest is here," said the gray bird. "It is comfortable and waits to hold you in your slumber."

"You may keep the nest," said the scarlet bird. "I only wish you peace. I will seek rest on another branch and wait for first light."

"But there is seed inside this window," said the gray bird. "If you will rest here, I will bring it out to you in the morning, and together we will sing the song of first light."

"You may keep the seed," said the scarlet bird. "I only wish you peace. In the morning I will gather under bush and tree as I have always done."

"I am sad," said the gray, "that you will not keep the bargain. For an agreement means to both give and receive. I cannot make you use this nest, nor can I make you eat my master's seed, but I have not yet given you the secret of rest, and that I must do before you fly away.

"Come closer," said the collector bird, "for my tether keeps me close to the window. The secret must be told quietly, and you are too far away."

The scarlet bird looked away. The sky was dark except for the moon that watched her sleep each night. A cloud moved across the sky, and a cool breeze ruffled her feathers.

"A bargain is a bargain," said the gray bird.

The songbird leaned away. She almost took flight but stopped. Instead, she leaned in close to the gray bird to hear the secret.

An agreement means to both give and receive.

With a single peck to the head, the collector bird killed the songbird.

In the morning, the master came out into his garden. Above him the gray bird sang the song of first light. The notes were true. If the spirit was less, the master knew that he could have nothing better from a bird tethered to his house.

Carefully the master took the body of the scarlet bird. He put the bird in a mahogany box. He dug a small grave and laid the box inside. At the head of the grave, he put an elegant silver marker much like the many other silver markers that lined the edge of his garden.

When the song and burial were done, the master took seed and strands and walked up to the room where the gray bird was tethered. He fed and doted on the gray collector bird.

He dearly loved the fat, gray bird. No other bird would wear such a tether.

How, then, would he hear such beautiful songs?

The End

Acknowledgements

The Bethlehem Writers Group, LLC acknowledges with gratitude the contributions of the Guest Judges for our 2019 and 2020 Short Story Award competitions. John Grogan, international bestselling author of *Marley & Me*, served as judge of our 2019 Short Story Award competition selecting "Oranges and Roses" by Angela Albertson. Peter Abrahams (also writing as Spencer Quinn), bestselling author of the Chet and Bernie series, among others, served as judge of our 2020 Short Story Award competition selecting "Hubbard Had a Fancy Bra," by Brett Wolff. Both stories appear in this volume. The time and experience these authors shared with us is greatly appreciated.

We also wish to thank BWG member Dianna Sinovic for donating her time and editorial skills to help make our stories as free from errors as is humanly possible.

About the Authors

Angela Albertson is the winner of the 2019 Bethlehem Writers Roundtable Short Story Award. She is a university student and equestrian who has a deep appreciation for all animals. She strives to help people understand the complex connections between themselves and the creatures of this earth. Angela organizes her days and life around her horses and other assortment of animals, and, in the quiet moments, she'll tell herself stories and develop fantastical worlds inside her head. In her spare time, she can be found writing down these stories or curled up enjoying a book. Angela intends to continue to improve her writing and to one day write children's literature. For now, she's focusing on finishing her bachelor's degree with a double minor in kinesiology and creative writing.

Courtney Annicchiarico has lived in the Lehigh Valley for the past fifteen years, but will always be a Jersey Girl at heart. Previous publications include stories in various BWG anthologies.

Jeff Baird is a career educator at the secondary and post graduate level teaching teachers how to integrate technology into their classrooms. He has presented at numerous state and national technology conferences such as Tetradata National Training Conference and Pennsylvania Educational Technology Conference (PETE&C) http://slideplayer.

com/slide/8405554/ and has published in the field of educational technology. He is the author of *Streamlining Response to Intervention Screening* (http://www.ascd.org/ascd-express/vol4/406-holben.aspx) and the subject of *Assess. Instruct. Repeat.* by Jennifer Demski (https://thejournal.com/rti). Lately, he has branched off into musings about hiking through Mother Nature, particularly those with waterfalls or mountain vistas, with his trusty canine companion, a rescued German Shorthaired Pointer. He resides in the beautiful Lehigh Valley of Pennsylvania where he is a contributing member of the Bethlehem Writers Group. His short stories appear in all the previous "Sweet, Funny, and Strange" anthologies from the Bethlehem Writers Group, LLC. You can find him at his Amazon author page at https://www.amazon.com/Jeff-Baird/e/B0033URREQ%3Fref=dbs_a_mng_rwt_scns_share and his website at www.jeffbaird.net

PETER J BARBOUR has been writing for over 30 years. He published a memoir, "Loose Ends," in 1987. He most enjoys creating short fiction. His stories have appeared in Short-Story.me, StoryStar.com, *Rue Scribe, Piker Press, ARTPOST Magazine*, and *The Starlit Path*. He wrote and illustrated two children's books, *Gus at Work* (2016), *Oscar and Gus* (2019). He is the graduate of University of Pennsylvania where he completed his BA in biology. He attended Temple University School of Medicine and Stanford University Medical School where he completed a residency in Neurology. He practiced neurology in the Lehigh Valley until his retirement in 2015. He is married and enjoys travel and the outdoors. He believes what comes from the heart goes to the heart. Please visit his website at https://PeteBarbour.com.

JODI BOGERT considers herself a storyteller, not just a writer. Her goal in life is to release her debut novel and get published in her favorite literary magazines, such as *The Sun* and *One Story*. So far, she has written short stories and dabbled in blog-

About the Authors

ging and journalism. Still, there is much to pursue and accomplish in the future.

A. E. Decker has been a member of the Bethlehem Writers Group since 2011. A former ESL tutor and doll-maker turned writer of fantasy, her short stories have appeared in such magazines as *Beneath Ceaseless Skies*, *Fireside Magazine*, and *The Sockdolager* as well as in the BWG's own anthology, *Once Around the Sun*, which she helped edit. Her YA novels in the Moonfall Mayhem series include *The Falling of the Moon*, *The Meddlers of Moonshine*, and *Into the Moonless Night*, all from World Weaver Press. Like all writers, she is owned by three cats.

Marianne H. Donley writes fiction from short stories to funny romances and quirky murder mysteries. She makes her home in Tennessee with her husband and son. She is a member of Bethlehem Writers Group, Romance Writers of America, Music City Romance Writers, Sisters in Crime, and Charmed Writers.

Ralph Hieb enjoys reading and writing paranormal fiction. He resides in Bethlehem, PA, with his wife Nancy. The couple enjoys travel and makes a point each year to take a trip to someplace they have never seen before. In addition to BWG, Ralph is a member of the Greater Lehigh Valley Writers Group where he has served as president and a member representative on the board of directors.

DT Krippene deserted aspirations of being a biologist to live the corporate dream and raise a family. After six homes, a ten-year stint working in Asia, and an imagination that never slept, his muse refused to be hobbled as a mere dream. DT writes science fiction, dystopian, parallel-world fantasy, and paranormal. His short story, "Hell of a Deal," appears in the BWG anthology *Untethered*, and he was a twice-featured author in *Bethlehem Writers Roundtable* with "Snowbelt Sanctuary" and "In Simple Terms." His current project is set in a near-future dystopia where over 95% of the human population has been wiped out by a virus, and survivors are unable to procreate . . . until a small number of women give birth on the same day. You can find DT at his blog, "Searching for Light in the Darkness" at: https://dtkrippene.com

JEROME W. MCFADDEN has been writing fiction for the past several years. His stories have appeared in various fiction magazines and e-zines, such as *Flash Fiction Offensive, Over My Dead Body, Eclectic Flash Fiction,* and *Bethlehem Writers Roundtable*. Many of his favorites are included in his book *Off the Rails: A Collection of Weird, Wicked, & Wacky Stories* published in 2019. It placed as a finalist for both the 2020 Next Generation Indie Book Awards and the National Indie Excellence Awards. He received a Second Place Bullet Award for the best crime fiction to appear on the web in June, 2011, and has had his short stories performed aloud on the stage by the Liar's League in London and the Liar's League in Hong Kong. His stories have appeared in various anthologies, including *Hardboiled: Crime Scene, Once Around the Sun, A Christmas Sampler, A Readable Feast,* and *Let It Snow*. He has also won honorable mentions in Writer's Digest Magazine annual national fiction awards, as well as in several regional writing contests.

EMILY P. W. MURPHY is a writer and freelance editor. Her short stories appear in *A Christmas Sampler: Sweet, Funny, and Strange Holiday Tales, Once Around the Sun: Sweet, Funny, and Strange Tales for All Seasons, A Readable Feast: Sweet, Funny, and Strange Tales for Every Taste, Once Upon a Time: Sweet, Funny, and Strange Tales for All Ages,* and *Untethered: Sweet, Funny, and Strange Tales of the Paranormal,* among other publications. After growing up in Pennsylvania, she has relocated to the Baltimore, MD area with her husband Adam, their two children, and their three cats. Visit Emily's website at: EmilyPWMurphy.com

About the Authors

CHRISTOPHER D. OCHS' foray into writing began in 2014 with his epic fantasy *Pindlebryth of Lenland*. Using his skills learned with Greater Lehigh Valley Writers Group, BWG, and the Lehigh Valley Storytelling Guild, he crafted a collection of mirthful macabre short stories, *If I Can't Sleep, You Can't Sleep*, and short fiction in two of BWG's anthologies, *Once Upon a Time* and *Untethered*. His latest work is a gritty, YA, urban fantasy/horror, *My Friend Jackson*. He has too many interests outside of writing for his own good. With previous careers in physics, engineering, and software, and his incessant dabblings as a CGI animator, classical organist, and voice talent, it's a wonder he can remember to pay the dog and feed his bills. Wait, what?

DIANNA SINOVIC writes fiction in her off-hours. She has been an editor for most of her career, and currently manages a team of writers and editors for a marketing company that focuses on healthcare information. She's originally from Kansas City, MO, but now lives in Upper Bucks County with her husband. When she's not writing, you can find her hiking or paddling her kayak or canoe. In the realm of fiction, Dianna writes short stories in several genres. She is a member of Sisters in Crime, the Horror Writers Association, the American Medical Writers Association, and the Bethlehem Writers Group, LLC.

DIANE SISMOUR lives with her husband at the foothills of the Blue Mountain range in Eastern Pennsylvania. When she's not checking guests into her Leaser Lake B & B, or supervising a cleaning crew at construction sites for Sismour's Janitorial Co., she's writing poetry, suspense, psychological horror, and romantic comedy short stories and novels. She is a member of Romance Writers of America, Liberty States Fiction Writers, the Horror Writers Association, and Bethlehem Writers Group, LLC. Diane advocates helping others as those who have aided her along her journey by giving writing workshops and as a motivational speaker for Women-Owned Small Businesses.

Fur, *Feathers*, and Scales

Kidd Wadsworth is still searching for a career. But maybe most of all, Kidd is searching for God. While looking within herself for the inner light, she found people living magical lives in the hidden castles of her mind, screaming to be heard. So, she writes, peering behind commas and under subplots for the One she knows is calling to her.

Paul Weidknecht is the author of *Native to This Stream: Brief Writings About Fly-Fishing & the Great Outdoors*. His work has appeared in *Gray's Sporting Journal, Outdoor Life, Rosebud,* and *Shenandoah,* among others. He has won the Lodestone Prize for Short Fiction and the Peter Barry Short Story Competition and has been awarded a scholarship to The Norman Mailer Writers Colony. His short script, "Driven," won the Let's Make It! Screenwriting Competition and is currently in pre-production in Romania. He lives in New Jersey.

Brett Wolff is the winner of the 2020 Bethlehem Writers Roundtable Short Story Award. He is a part-time trial attorney and full-time legal writer, perpetually in the middle of at least three new short stories. He has run ultra marathons around the globe, won a national championship in trial advocacy, and performed on stage doing mildly amusing stand-up comedy, thickly enunciated Shakespeare, and deeply Americanized British farce. He graduated with a Bachelor's degree in Philosophy and Political Science from Vanderbilt University and a Juris Doctorate from Loyola Law School (L.A.). He lives in Sierra Madre, California with his spouse and fellow published author debating proper use of the em dash and new hydration strategies.

Carol L. Wright escaped a career in law and academia for one in writing mysteries and more. She loves creating her Gracie McIntyre Mysteries where, unlike in life, justice always prevails. The first in the series, *Death in Glenville Falls,* was a finalist for both a Killer Nashville Silver Falchion Award and a Next Generation Indie Book Award. She also writes short

About the Authors

stories that have appeared in award-winning literary journals and anthologies. Her latest, "Method for Murder," appears in the *Malice Domestic 15: Mystery Most Theatrical*. She has collected some of her favorite short stories in the book *A Christmas on Nantucket and Other Stories*. She is married to her college sweetheart and they live in the Lehigh Valley of Pennsylvania with their rescue dog and clowder of cats. Learn more at her website: CarolLWright.com.

WILL WRIGHT Being raised by great parents and having an amazing sister, Will Wright is a lucky guy. He's also been fortunate to be included in many Bethlehem Writers Group anthologies over the years. Other stories by Will can be found on the blog, Junk Drawer (https://gofigurereads.blogspot.com). His fantasy novel, Cinder, is available on Amazon and Smashwords. Will lives in Winston-Salem, NC.

CPSIA information can be obtained
at www.ICGtesting.com
Printed in the USA
BVHW050620090223
657947BV00001B/2